S0-BTB-243

SWEPT AWAY!

The cabin quaked and rumbled, the blasting sound growing louder as the water cannon fired their jets at a point just below the top of the bluff.

"What now, Ben?"

"We get out of here and back to town. Then we keep looking, at least for a while. If you're willing, at least."

"And if we don't find her?"

The roaring was growing louder, the cabin beginning to shake and shiver, making strange, twisting, straining noises . . . but Ben hardly noticed.

He saw the look on Andy's face, the fear that rose suddenly in his eyes, the opening of the mouth to scream, but the scream was never heard. Something struck the cabin that felt like the very fist of God, slamming the base of it, ripping it asunder and pushing it up and back, the course suddenly reversing as the cabin, blasted loose by a stray blast from one of the water cannon, now spilling out and down, pitching over the edge of the bluff and tumbling, turning, crashing down the slope into the white hell of water and stone below, carrying its two screaming human occupants with it.

Other *Leisure* books by Will Cade:
FLEE THE DEVIL

THE GALLOWSMAN

WILL CADE

LEISURE BOOKS NEW YORK CITY

To Don D'Auria, with appreciation

A LEISURE BOOK®

November 1998

Published by

Dorchester Publishing Co., Inc.
276 Fifth Avenue
New York, NY 10001

ISBN 0-8439-4452-8

The name "Leisure Books" and the stylized "L" with design are trademarks of Dorchester Publishing Co., Inc.

Printed in the United States of America.

THE
GALLOWSMAN

Chapter One

With stage fare at two bits a mile, he couldn't afford to
ride, and so he walked, with the single feed sack containing
his entire worldly fortune slung over his shoulder. He was
not happy to be afoot. Usually he enjoyed walking, but that
was in the lowlands, where a man could breathe and enjoy
some benefit from it. Here in the high Colorado mountains,
every breath seemed thin, empty of sustenance and unable
to satisfy.

Pausing for what seemed the hundredth time to let his
gasping subside, he felt much older than his forty years. As
he stood panting, he examined an odd heap beside the road-
way, which was still partly covered with snow despite the
spring season. A dead mule. Another beast worked to death
hauling heavy mining and smelting equipment up these
mountain roads in this cussedly thin atmosphere. How
many dead mules was that? Twelve, he believed, since he'd
started keeping count in this endless hike up toward Ferguson.

When he had his wind back, he shifted the canvas sack
to his other shoulder and set out again. The road still

climbed, but leveled somewhat ahead. Nearing the crest at last! Once beyond that, he would see the town of Ferguson, newest of Colorado's silver boomtowns, and a destination Ben Woolard looked forward to with a combination of unfamiliar hope and all-too-familiar dread.

A sound behind him made him turn. A wagon came up past the dead mule and toward him. A tall, broadly built black man drove it, and flashed a big grin at Ben as he neared.

Ben grinned back, being friendly, but also because he was amused: The wagon driver's teeth flashed like the palace of Midas. Every tooth in his head, or at least every tooth that showed, had been capped over in bright gold.

"Howdy," Ben said.

"Hello, sir," the cheerful driver said, pulling his mules to a halt, studying Ben for a moment. Apparently Ben passed his test. "Can I offer you a ride?"

"You can, and I accept."

The driver reached down, took Ben's sack, and Ben climbed into the seat beside him. "Hard thing, keeping your wind here in the mountains, until you get used to it," the driver said.

"It shows on me that much, huh?"

"Shows in every newcomer, sir. This is a different world up here among these peaks than what's lived in down below."

"My name's Woolard," Ben said, putting out his hand for a shake. "Ben Woolard. Mighty obliged for the ride."

"Woolard! Well, that's a name well-knowed in Ferguson. There's a Jake Woolard there who owns him a big store and a sleeping house and some other stuff. Mine stock, too. Doing mighty well for himself."

"Jake Woolard is my brother," Ben said.

"No! I be! Well, sir, that's really something! You and Mr. Jake are brothers!"

"What's your name?"

"Roanie, sir. Roanie Platt."

"You a miner, Roanie?"

"Me? No, sir. Mostly I work for myself, sir, me and my

8

brother together. We haul stuff about in wagons, anything that needs hauling. And we drive ore wagons, too, for one of the smelters there in town, every now and then." He pointed ahead. "Look yonder. You can see the town now."

Ben could smell it, too. A smoky, heavy smell in the thin air, the stench of smelters mixing their noxious fumes with the cooksmoke of hundreds of rough chimneys. Ben studied the town as it gleamed in the sunlight beneath the bench of low-lying smoke.

A yellowish pallor marked the irregular jumble of buildings that comprised Ferguson. Ben couldn't account for the distinctive coloration at first. As the wagon rumbled nearer, he figured it out: The yellow was that unique hue of unpainted pine lumber, the predominant building material of Ferguson. So new was most of the town that the yellow of the boards had yet to be weathered away.

Ben squinted as the wagon circled around a bend in the road. "Where's the streets?" he asked Roanie.

"There ain't nothing of what you could rightly call a proper street, sir," he replied. "Except for Center Street. Right there it runs through the heart of town, and you can see that somebody's throwed up a hut right in the middle of it, but it won't last. The town commission'll have that pulled down right swift. All the rest of the town is kind of just built wherever, you see—no real pattern to it, nothing but alleys and trails and such instead of streets. You know much about the town, sir?"

"Not much. Used to be a placer-mining town, I believe."

"That's right, yes, sir. Them was the gold days, back before the town even had a real name. You can still find old cabins and huts all through the hills where the gold miners lived. And the pressure cannons south of town— see them? there?—still uncover some of the old places that got buried under slides and such since the old days."

Ben gazed with interest at the pressure cannon, which to his disappointment were not operating at the moment. He'd read about the devices: big pipelines that brought water down from the peaks, narrowing all the way, so that when the heavy water reached the narrow nozzle openings, it was under enough pressure to blast away stone and soil like so much dust. The pressure cannon were the last vestige of the gold-mining days of this community. Day by day the cannon blasted through dirt and rock that had been panned by placer miners years before, and day by day the pressure miners were rewarded by the discovery of gold that had escaped the earlier, less technologically advanced miners. But even so, it was all a mere shadow of the old and lost glory days of gold; the color of primary wealth found in these mountains these days had a silvery sheen.

Ben turned his eyes back to the town. It sat on a slight slope, surrounded on all sides by hills and high mountains. He'd never seen such a shapeless farrago of structures. Among the predominant pine buildings he now made out as many tents and frame-and-canvas structures, as well as countless log huts and cabins. An improvised town, this one, a grown-up version of a child's tiny city of upturned crates and boxes, but with less order.

"Yes, sir," Roanie went on. "This place wouldn't be what it is now if there'd only been the gold. Most of that was gone long ago. It was the carbonate, with the silver in it, that caused this town to be. One of the first of the gold miners is who figured out that there was more fortune to be made from the silver than the gold. It was his boy, in fact, who the town's named after. Poor boy. Poor little Ferguson Jones!"

"Why 'poor little Ferguson'?"

"Well, the little fellow died, that's why. Partly because of his father getting so worked up when he found out there was silver to be had. The little boy, maybe eight or nine years old, was sickly, they say, and his father stayed too long up here instead of going down to the lower lands when the winter begun coming in. He tried to leave too late, and a snowbank fell and caught his boy. Smothered the life out of him before they could dig him out. The father, Chance Jones, named the town Ferguson in memory of his child. I think it'd have been better if he'd named the town after

10

hisself. Chance. It'd be a good name for a mining town. 'Come take your chances at Chance.' "

"Sad story. About the little boy dying, I mean."

"Yes, sir, it is. And there's plenty of other sad stories in this town. Folks come in thinking they'll make it big and rich real fast, but a lot wind up going broke, or getting hurt or killed some way or another. There's a graveyard east of the town, and I know the fellows who dig the holes. They keep three or four holes dug ahead, knowing there'll be need for them before long, and sure enough, they'll have them holes filled before they've been there two days. Every time."

"Dangerous place, this town?"

"Dangerous enough. And no good law. None that's lasted, anyhow. There's a town marshal, but he don't do squat. Spends most his time prospecting. And who can blame him? Why would anybody come to a town and risk his skin fighting drunks and thieves and shooters and such for what little bit a peace officer gets paid, when instead he can go out and dig him a hole or two, and maybe strike it rich?"

They rolled into the town itself. Ben examined the mob of humanity there, mostly young, male, and unkempt. A dirtier rabble he'd not seen since the war.

"All these folks miners?" he asked as Roanie weaved a course down the milling, crowded street.

"Most. But not all. See that building there? Two lawyers operating in there. Yonder tent has a doctor, though as best I know there ain't but two doctors in town who went to no doctoring school. And there's plenty of merchants, all kinds, and dentists, and teamsters like me, and assayers . . . every kind of business you can think of, there's somebody here already trying to do it. And if there ain't already, there'll be two of them show up tomorrow to do it. What brings you to Ferguson, sir? You going to mine?"

Ben paused. "I've just come to work with my brother. I don't know just what I'll be doing, exactly."

They rolled on, deeper into town. Or was it a town at all? No railroad yet reached this place, and there was no sense of pattern and settlement that normally went with the concept of township. No, Ben decided, this was little more than an overgrown mining camp, a place were function overruled form, and beauty didn't matter a whit. The buildings were irregular, the boardwalks even more so. Signs were everywhere, offering two drinks for two bits, rooms for rent, laundry service, shoe shines, groceries. The street was a pitted expanse of trampled dirt, filled with horse droppings that were trod underfoot along with the mud.

"Hey!" Roanie declared abruptly. "Dang if it ain't my brother yonder! Hey, Billy!"

Ben saw the indicated man, a slightly smaller version of Roanie himself, seated on a keg on a street corner, head tilted back, mouth open, and another man working hard on his teeth. Only his eyes turned in response to Roanie's shout. He waved as best he could without moving.

Ben asked, "He's getting a tooth pulled?"

"No, sir, no sir, getting another tooth golded over ... like mine." He grinned his bright gold grin at Ben. "Billy's been jealous of my gold teeth since I got 'em done, and he's been having his own golded over, one at a time, as he can afford it."

"I never seen a dentist on a street corner before," Ben said.

"There's a lot in Ferguson you've likely never seen before," Roanie replied. "Like the buildings. This town lives in tents and cabins. Your brother's got one of the few real houses in the whole dang community. Big old porch on it, carpet on the floors, calico on the walls, muslin on the ceiling. Good furniture, too. Me and my brother hauled it in for him. He'd bought it in Denver. Your brother's done good for himself here, and it ain't took him long to do it."

"Jake's always got a way of making things work out."

"Yonder's a casino," Roanie said, pointing as the wagon made another turn and scattered a flock of chickens freely roaming the streets. "Casinos and smelters in this town got one thing in common: They both go 'round the clock, seven days a week."

"What's that place?" Ben asked, indicating a big, war-

ehouselike building to his left with a sign reading CATHE-
DRAL OF REST on its front. "Some kind of big funeral
place?"

"Lord, sir, no! That your own brother's sleeping house.
Smartest business in this town, if you ask me, which you
ain't."

"What's so smart about it?"

"One of the things that's hardest for a newcomer to find
in this town, sir, is a place to sleep. Men sleep wherever
they can—saloon floors, under boardwalks, in alleys, on
rooftops. I seen a whole family in a big crate behind a
grocery store just two days ago. But the best place for a
new man to go for his snores is the sleeping house."

"Looks like a storehouse to me."

"It's just a big old building, sir, with row and row of
bunks in it, two deep. You go in, pay your fifty cents for
the night, and you can sleep on a good mattress and with
a warm blanket. A lot better than a saloon floor, I can tell
you."

"You slept there?"

"No, sir, not me. I'm colored. I ain't allowed." He said
it matter-of-factly, a man accustomed to discrimination.
"Sir, is your brother expecting you at a spific time or
place?"

"No. He knows I'm coming, but not when. Where's his
house?"

"Not far. I can take you there, if you want."

"I'd appreciate it. But, Roanie . . . I'm a little short on
money. I feel I ought to pay you. . . ."

"No pay needed, sir. I'm glad to lend a hand. I ain't one
to let a man walk when I got room on my wagon."

"You're a kind man."

"Your brother will be pleased to see you come, I'll bet,"
Roanie said. "Me and my brother are close as we can be.
A brother's a fine thing to have. Yes, sir, he'll be happy to
see you show up."

Ben looked away. "I hope you're right."

* * *

13

Jake's house, like most things in Ferguson, wasn't much to look at.

Ben stood for a long time in the shade of a little grove of trees that had somehow escaped destruction as firewood, and studied his brother's home. Shaped like an L and only one story tall, it was distinctive only for being somewhat larger than the typical Ferguson hovel, and for its long porch.

Now that he was here, Ben was reluctant to make his presence known. He'd already swallowed much pride merely to accept his brother's invitation, and many times he'd come within a hairsbreadth of turning back during the long journey from St. Louis to here . . . but there had been nothing to turn back to.

He turned away, sighed, and meandered back into the town, onto Center Street, putting off for a while the actual moment of reunion. Wandering along, he eyed the many saloons, none of them fancy by any standard, but all of them offering the kind of liquid refreshment he'd certainly enjoy just now. But he couldn't. He'd struggled hard to break liquor's hold on his soul, and he wouldn't throw that away. Liquor belonged to a past that he was determined to let go . . . if only it would let go of him.

He stopped on the boardwalk, looking around. Ferguson, Colorado. A place of hope for those already here and the scores who arrived every day. Most came seeking their mortal salvation in the black carbonate ore that lay beneath the surface of this rugged land, others through the network of commerce that inevitably grew in a mining boomtown.

Ben Woolard, on the other hand, sought his salvation and reformation through his brother, the brother who had always seemed to succeed even as Ben inevitably failed.

He hadn't seen Jake in years. Funny thing. His own brother, to be met again this very day, and it felt like he was going to meet a stranger.

He roamed the street the rest of the day, watching the bustling activity all around, and did not turn his steps back toward the house of Jake Woolard until the sun dipped its lower edge below the highest of the peaks looming in the west above the town.

He was halfway to his destination when he realized he was being followed.

Chapter Two

A street robber, maybe. What he would later learn the folks of the Colorado mining towns called a "footpad." Ben increased his pace slightly and ducked around a trio of half-drunken miners coming his way on the boardwalk, and during the brief moments their big forms hid him from the man trailing him, ducked into the nearest alley and backed up against the wall.

The man passed the mouth of the alley a moment later and paused there, looking uncertainly up and down the street.

"Behind you," Ben said.

The young man, in his mid-twenties at most, jumped in his boots and cursed. Wheeling, he faced Ben.

"I do believe I know you," Ben said, stepping forward. "Andrew? Andy Woolard? Is it you?"

The young fellow shook off his look of startlement and replaced it with a smug and contemptuous expression. "Well! I *thought* that was you I saw roaming about, Ben."

"So I'm just plain Ben now, eh? No more 'Uncle Ben'?"

"I ain't a child no more, and I don't talk like one. I'm as much a grown man as you now." He smiled rather bitterly. "The folks tell me, matter of fact, that I look quite a lot like you." He eyed Ben up and down. "God, I hope not. You look like you've been through it and back again."

"I have. You know that story, I reckon."

"Oh, yes. I know. I've heard it all. And from what I've heard, it appears you and me are alike in more than looks." With that he reached beneath his coat and pulled out a flat metal flask, which he uncorked and swigged without breaking his gaze from Ben's.

Ben watched the young man drink and hoped to heaven that the fierce liquor-hunger the sight roused in him didn't show. He longed to reach out and grab that flask, put it to his own thirsty lips. . . .

Andrew Woolard recorked the flask and put it back into his pocket. "I do love my whiskey, Ben. Fine stuff. I hear you hold a similar point of view."

"I did. I've put it behind me now. It would have killed me."

"Could be worse ways to die."

"What's wrong, Andy? What's this crazy talk? Something bothering you?"

"Why did you come here?"

"Because your father invited me to."

"You've come to be his servant? Going to let brother take care of you?"

"I've come to do honest work for Jake, and I'll do a good job of it."

"Doing what? You going to wipe his butt for pay or something?"

"You got quite a smart mouth on you, don't you, son? If I didn't know better, I'd think maybe you weren't glad to see your old uncle."

Andy put on a fulsome look of shock. "Why, did I give you that notion? Forgive me! Why, I surely do hate you thought that!" He pulled out the flask again and took another slow, deliberate swig. Then he shoved the flask toward Ben. An invitation.

"No," Ben said. "I told you. I put that behind me."

Andy laughed. Ben wondered why. Andy put the flask away again—for good this time, Ben hoped.

"You'll be heading for the house now, I reckon," Andy said.

"Reckon I should."

"Pa won't be there. Ma will, and Judy. Judy's twelve years old now. Eats like a pig. Spends most her time stuffing her mouth."

"What about you, Andy? What do you spend your time doing these days?"

"Trying to drink myself to death. Want to join me?"

Ben didn't know what to say to that, so he didn't say anything. He turned and began striding down the boardwalk, toward Jake's house, having had quite enough of Andy.

Andy watched him go, then pulled the flask out for another drink. When Ben was out of sight, he sighed and turned the other way, heading for the nearest saloon.

Sally Woolard had been pretty as long as Ben had known her, but the years were finally beginning to leave their traces. Not as much, though, as on Ben himself; this he had detected by the quick look of shock when she'd first seen his craggy face in the light.

Now she and he were engaged in a rather forced conversation. When his eyes caught hers she smiled broadly and a bit too nonchalantly. Ben was making her nervous, obviously. He wished he'd lingered outside a little longer and not approached the house until after Jake came home.

Judy Woolard, meanwhile, seemed not at all discomfited by the presence of this long-absent uncle. She stared with the honest interest of the typical adolescent, eyeing him from the corner while nibbling on a plate of potatoes and bacon. A pretty girl, but tending toward heft. Ben recalled that Sally's family, whom he had met many years before at Jake's wedding, had several sizable members. Young Judith, namesake of her two-hundred-pound maternal grandmother, seemed destined to carry on the family tradition.

"So Jake's got some mining interest, does he?" Ben said, trying to advance a struggling conversation.

"Yes. Some. He's taken a lot of mine stock in trade for this or that, and he does some grubstaking. He owns little pieces of at least a score of mines. A few have struck, and a lot of the others look promising, he says."

"We're going to be rich," Judith said around a mouthful of potato. "We're going to move back to Denver someday and build a mansion."

"Hush, Judy!" her mother remonstrated. "We don't know that we're going to be rich. And we don't need a mansion in Denver—we're doing quite well here."

"Very nice house you got," Ben exaggerated. "Very nice. One of the best in town, from what I saw."

"Thank you. It's not that much, really. Anywhere else but Ferguson, and it wouldn't look at all special. Among a bunch of cabins and glorified tents, it seems much more than it is."

"Better than what I've lived in the past couple of years," Ben said.

"Tell me, Ben . . . are you well now?"

"If you mean have I gotten over being a drunkard, yes, I have. Oh, I still want the whiskey as much as ever. The difference now is, I don't drink it."

"Never?"

"Never."

She smiled at him. "I'm so glad. It must mean you've been able to finally get over your losses and sorrows."

"I haven't gotten over anything. I never will. All I've gotten over is trying to drown it all away in whiskey. Doesn't work, you know."

He was seated at the kitchen table, leaning on his elbows with his hands clasped before him as she busied herself around in tasks he knew were undertaken merely to keep a comfortable space between them. Now, however, she stopped and came to the table herself, and took a seat across from him.

"I'm sorry I never got to meet her," she said. "She was pretty?"

20

"Beautiful."

"And the children too, I'm sure."

He blinked. It hurt terribly to think about Molly, even worse to think about the children. Three grand, lovely children, a dear and affectionate wife, prettiest woman he had ever known . . . and all of them gone. Buried in Kentucky. And buried with them, the best part of Ben Woolard's life.

"They were all wonderful children. Very dear to me."

"Measles, was it?"

"Yes."

"It's awful."

Ben looked at her with eyes encircled by lines and shadows that hadn't been there the last time she had seen him so many years before. "It is awful. And the worst of it, the pure hell of it for me, is that it was me who brought the disease to them. Me. I caught it, suffered out the fever and the spots, and lived. They caught it, one by one . . . and died. One by one."

Sally's eyes filled with tears. A sympathetic woman, even if almost a stranger to him. She said nothing because there was nothing to say. Over in the corner, Judith had stopped eating and stared in silence.

"I lived and they died. Why? It's that that drove me to the bottle. Asking why. Asking again and again, and never getting an answer."

"Ben, I . . . I just want you to know that . . . Oh, Ben, I don't know what to say. I wish it had never happened."

"Me too."

She brightened by an effort of will, and beamed a smile at him with tears still in her eyes. "But things will be better now that you're here!" she said chipperly. "Jake will get you work, grubstake you if you want to mine, lend you a hand until you can find the kind of situation that suits you, and you can start building a new life for yourself. Here with us. You'll see how good it can be after Jake shows you around the town. There's such opportunity here, Ben! Why, there's people who come to this town as paupers, get themselves a grubstake from people like Jake, and before you know it, they're running a successful mine. Happens all the time! And the beauty of it is, a novice has as much chance at a silver strike as a veteran prospector. There's a layer of ore underlying this whole region, Jake says, and it's just a matter of sinking a shaft at the right place and to the right depth. Sometimes the ore is right at the surface! Why, there've been a few who have turned over a shovel three or four times and struck wealth!''

"Is being a miner what Jake has in mind for me?"

She opened her mouth to answer but never got the chance. The front door burst open so suddenly that Ben came to his feet and barely stifled a shout of alarm, as through his mind flashed vivid and well-remembered scenes of fire and lead and uniformed men in blue and gray and butternut screaming as death claimed them. . . .

It was Andy who had come in. "Mother! My dear old ma!" he bellowed, voice slurred. He was raging drunk. "Dear old mother who bore me in her own body! And, why, looky here—it's *Uncle Ben*!" The emphasis on the last two words dripped with sarcasm. "Old Uncle Ben, the Woolard who tried to drink himself to death and failed!" He reached under his coat and pulled out that familiar flask once again. "Here's to you, Uncle Ben, from the Woolard who's trying to drink himself to death and—unlike you— will succeed!"

"Andy!" Sally yelled, rising. "Andy, for God's sake— how dare you . . ."

He had turned up the flask, but there was nothing in it. He made a wry face and put on a show of peering into the flask's mouth, shaking his head.

Judith, hugging her plate over in the corner, quietly began to cry.

"Andy, I won't have you in here like this. I won't have you in this house drunk!"

"Why, are you throwing me out, Ma? What, there room for only one drunk at a time in this fine dwelling? Has dear pitiful old Uncle Ben taken my place as the family charity project?"

"Andy, get out of this house! Get out before your father comes home!"

22

"Why? You think he might get mad at his little Andy? His bad little boy?"

"Andy, your uncle has come and he is a guest in our house, and I expect you to show the sort of respect that—"

"Oh, Uncle Ben and I met earlier today, on the street," Ben said. "Didn't he tell you? Why, we had the best talk, and sat down together for some of the finest whiskey to be found in all Colorado!"

"Sally, it's not true," Ben said. "I did meet Andy earlier, but there was no drinking. Not on my part, at least. I didn't tell you I met him because of . . . well, he was half drunk and rude as could be at the time."

Judith dropped her plate from her lap and turned her face away toward the wall. Andy, meanwhile, put his hand to his head as if it hurt suddenly, and winced. He turned and left the house without another word, the sarcasm and fire all at once gone from him.

Ben Woolard wondered just what kind of household he had come to. A troubled one, to be sure. Obviously he wasn't the only Woolard with a full share of problems.

When Andy was gone, several uncomfortable moments of silence followed. Sally turned a pallid face to Ben, opening her mouth to say something, but somehow failing to find words.

"It's all right," Ben said. "I reckon my nephew ain't glad to see me."

"It's . . . it's more than that," she said. "There's things that have happened. Troubles that Andy has had. Bad things that have come his way, and made him all angry and bitter."

The door opened again, not so loudly or suddenly this time. Ben turned and, for the first time in many a year, looked into the face of his elder brother.

Chapter Three

Ben would later ponder why his first sight of Jake after so long a separation took him back not to the last time he and his brother were together, but all the way to a time of an ending war in the Federally occupied city of Nashville, Tennessee, and a view of his brother that had ingrained itself as a recurring memory: Jake, then a uniformed new veteran of the 12th Kentucky Cavalry, standing on a corner of High Street, nervous but trying not to show it, and looking handsome as the devil. He was waiting to enter the courthouse and give testimony in a military trial that for a time made him famous in the region. Ben had been involved in that trial, too, far more deeply than his brother. He, too, had become briefly famous.

Ben, more than any other man who testified in that trial, was responsible for the aftermath of it, in which an infamous and shadowy figure of war went to a prison-yard gallows and died with the jerk of a noosed rope, a macabre smile on his face even as the trap dropped. When it was done, Jake had turned and said to no one in particular, "Well, it's finished, then."

The memory passed, and Ben saw Jake as he was: much older, thicker around the middle and thinner in the hair, and with a look of surprise on his face that erupted into a smile.

"Ben? *Ben!*" He came forward, arms spreading, and Ben went to him, grinning like a fool. The brotherly embrace that followed was long and crushing.

"Ben, by gum, you've made it at last! I've wondered every day when you'd arrive!"

"Took me a while, but I finally did."

"So you did. So you did. Sally, why didn't you send word out to me that Ben had come in? I'd have come home early if I'd . . . Sally? What's wrong?" He'd just noticed his wife's distraught expression, and his eyes shifted as well over to Judith, who huddled in the corner, looking scared.

"It's Andy again," she said. "He came in, in a very bad way. He was rude, disrespectful to me and to Ben . . . awful. He was awful."

Jake grew sober, glanced at Ben, obviously embarrassed that his brother's initial reunion with his only living close kin had been far from flawless. "In a bad way, you say . . . drunk?"

"Yes. Very."

Jake spoke apologetically to his brother. "Ben . . . I'm sorry for whatever bad things you've seen here. We're having some trouble out of Andy."

"I surmised that."

"I'm embarrassed. I'd hoped for your arrival to be a happy time."

"Well, I am happy. Surely happy to see you, Jake. And Sally and Judy have been nice as can be while we've waited on you to get back."

Jake grinned. "Good. Good. Well, I'll have to deal with Andy for how he's behaved, but in the meantime let's forget about it. My brother's here! And to stay, I hope."

"To stay . . . if you want me to. If there's proper work for me. I'll not stand for being a burden to you."

"No, you won't be. For one thing sure is true about this town: There's work for any man who wants it. Any man

26

who wants to can make his own work with a pick and a mule.''

"Sally's told me some about you and your success. I'm impressed.'' Ben smiled. "I'm glad one of the Woolard brothers has made something good and worthy of himself.''

"There's *two* good and worthy Woolard brothers, by gum, and I'll hear nothing to the contrary. But one of those brothers has suffered some hard blows in his life, worse than any man should, and he's had a rough go of it because of it.'' He spoke the next words very deliberately and with force: "A rough go that has now come to an end.''

"I hope that's true. I've made some bad decisions in my time, and I don't deny that now. I want to make good ones from here on out.'' Abruptly, tears rose in Ben's eyes, and it was his turn to feel embarrassed. "Jake, I want you to know, I appreciate the fine thing you're doing for me. Offering me work, a home—a man like me don't deserve it.''

"Nonsense. Every man deserves a chance to make the best of himself. That's what this growing nation of ours is all about. And if what you say is true, about wanting to make good choices and a better way for yourself, then, by gum, you've come to the best town in the nation for it. There's opportunity here, Ben. True opportunity. A man can get rich here by digging a hole! How many places can that be said about, huh?''

"Reckon not many.''

"So how was your travel? Enjoyable?''

"Mostly. Less so the farther up into these mountains that I came. There's some mighty thin air up here for a low-lander. If I hadn't caught me a wagon ride I'd probably still be out there huffing toward town, stopping to rest every five steps.''

"Who'd you ride in with?''

"Colored man with a mouth full of gold teeth. Name of Roanie something-or-other.''

"Oh, yes! I've seen that fellow. Roanie Platt. I believe he's got a gold-toothed brother, too.''

"He knew who you were right off,'' Ben said. "Declared you a prominent and powerful man.''

"I've done well enough, I suppose. You'll do well here, too. You and me have a lot of talking to do this evening, Ben."

Sally cut in. "What about Andy? Aren't you going to do something about him? He was . . . *awful!*"

Jake turned stern. "Andy is a grown man now. Even if he doesn't act like one. I'll not spend this night poking through every saloon and dive in town, trying to find him when he doesn't even want to be found. Especially not now that Ben is here."

She looked sad. Ben felt sorry for her, a mother grieving for a son obsessed, for whatever reason, with ruining himself, even destroying himself.

"You'll be wanting your supper now," Sally said to her husband.

"I'm starved. Ben, you eaten yet?"

"Sally fed me well."

"Come sit with me while I have my supper, then, and after that we'll have some cigars and good talk. You still like cigars, don't you?"

"Love 'em."

"Good. Good." Jake went over to where Judith still sat, and rumpled her hair with his hand. "How you, Punkin?"

"Andy acted real bad," she said.

"I know. I know. I'll be dealing with him soon. Don't you worry."

He sat down at the table as Sally loaded a plate for him. Grinning at Ben, shaking his head as if in pleasant disbelief that he was really there, he was a man Ben might envy. If not for the shadow cast onto this household by the troubled Andy Woolard, Ben could have perceived his brother as the world's most fortunate man.

The hour was late; Sally and Judith were asleep in their beds. Andy had not come home, but Jake wasn't particularly disturbed by this, telling Ben that Andy was seldom home anymore, spending nights with drinking companions, in cheap rooms, on saloon floors, and likely as not, in the cribs and chambers of the kind of fallen women that Ferguson, like any mining town, possessed in abundance.

"He said some troubling things to me today," Ben confided. "He talked like someone trying to kill himself slowly—and I know that kind of man well, having been one myself not all that long ago."

"Andy has suffered a hard blow, and it's left him very changed. Very hurt."

"May I ask what kind of blow it was?"

"One rather similar to yours, now that I think about it," Jake replied. "He was engaged to be married last year, and lost her."

"She left him?"

"She died. Killed. And the worst of it was, Andy was the one who killed her."

"What?"

"It was accidental. A shooting. A rifle he'd just bought. Somehow, when he laid it on a tabletop, it fell, and fired when it hit the floor. He hadn't even known the blasted thing was loaded. The bullet struck her in the side. She lingered for two weeks, suffering very terribly, before she died. Andy blames himself."

"He shouldn't. It wasn't his fault."

"No. No more than it was your fault you happened to be the first in your family to catch the measles."

"I know. It wasn't my fault . . . but it *feels* like it was. Same way Andy feels, I guess."

"Andy's following the same course you did. Liquor, self-destruction. I worry for him. His mother worries all the more. It's destroying her, right along with Andy."

"I gather that Andy resents me," Ben said. "Just some things he said when I first saw him today."

"I'm sure he does. You remind him of what he's doing to himself. Because despite all his talk about wanting to drink himself to death, I don't believe he really wants to. He wants to be pulled out of it, somehow, but now he's in so deep he doesn't know how to get back out again. And then you show up, a man who by all rights should have died long ago, the way you drank and such, yet you've made it through alive. He ought to see you as inspiration, but I suspect that right now, you're just someone to be envied.''

Ben chuckled ironically. "I'd have never thought anybody could find anything in me to envy."

They talked another hour, the topic shifting to Ben and his own difficult experiences—the good times that turned bad with the death of his family, the liquor that almost consumed him, and Jake's last-ditch bid to save his brother's life by offering him work and a new chance if only he'd shake off the whiskey and come join him in Ferguson. In Ferguson, Jake had promised, opportunity would be handed to Ben. He'd have a place, work, a hope and promise. But only if he'd cast off the liquor. Only if he'd come to Ferguson on his own, when he was ready, as a show of evidence that he was serious about wanting to reform.

The conversation dipped farther into the past, back into their Kentucky boyhood, the days of hunting, working the farm, racing their horses across the bluegrass countryside. The companions, the girlfriends, the youthful carousing. Good days. Good memories.

Then darker times, a few years past the boyhood joys. Hard and grim days of war. Two brothers joining the Union cavalry, making excellent showings for themselves as soldiers. Then the special service they had been called into, covert work that had taken Ben down into Tennessee and into the heart of a bushwhacker-infested region, his commission being to infiltrate a particular bushwhacker's band, to gather damning facts, evidence worthy of a military courtroom. . . .

Hard times, those. Dangerous times. But Ben Woolard, obedient soldier, had fulfilled his assignment. Working with his own brother Jake as his secret contact, he had filtered intelligence out to the Union military. When at last the bloody bushwhacker named Henry Champion was brought to trial in a Nashville courtroom, Ben had faithfully testified, unveiling the evidence he had gathered, the things he had witnessed and heard, while glint-eyed Henry Champion sat glaring at the young man he had thought was a fellow reb bushwhacker, an underling and follower, but who in fact was a Judas, betraying him to those who would see him killed.

Ben talked quietly about that episode of his life, so distant now in his experience, and seldom thought about any longer.

"You know, Jake," he said as he took the last puff from his third cigar of the night, "I recollect how I felt when Champion was finally hanged. It was odd, really. I felt kind of sorry for him, for I'd ridden with him and got to know him. Even to like him, sometimes . . . what rare part of him there was to like. But I was also relieved to know he was dead. The way he looked at me while I testified . . . I knew that he'd kill me, if he could, for what I was doing to him. He'd have killed me like I'd seen him kill so many others."

Jake, rolling his own cigar around in his mouth, stared at the wall and said nothing.

"Looking back now, I have trouble believing I actually did what I did," Ben went on. "To think I actually became part of a reb bushwhacker gang! Rode with them. Helped them rob folks, burn houses. But never did I kill anyone for them. That I wouldn't have done, though I tell you my heart was in my throat every day for fear Champion would call on me to prove my worth and loyalty by killing somebody at his behest. But it never happened. Thank God. It was always Champion or one of his higher followers who pulled the trigger or tied the noose. But even then, it haunted me. Standing by, watching men and even boys killed by that murdering scoundrel . . . and me doing nothing. Not that I was supposed to do anything—my charge was to observe and gather evidence, not to interfere. But I remember how many died, and how bad they died. You know what I'm talking about, Jake. You know how many I told you about personally, and you heard me give testimony. You even gave testimony yourself."

"I did, yes."

"He hated you too, you know. He hated everyone who testified against him. It's a good thing for me and you both that he was hanged."

"Yes. It is." Jake lifted his head sharply. "Listen! Did you hear that?"

Jake's sudden motion had startled Ben, lulled as he was by rich cigar smoke and reverie. "I didn't hear anything."

"Outside . . . something . . ."

Jake rose and went to the door. Ben felt a pins-and-needles edginess that he hoped didn't show. He'd been so lost in thought about long-ago days of espionage among Civil War bushwhackers that he caught himself halfway fearing that Jake would open that door and reveal the living phantom of Henry Champion himself, back from the dead to punish the two brothers whose work had helped spur him to the gallows.

Ben felt foolish, of course, when the open door revealed nothing but the passed-out form of Andy Woolard, curled up like an oversize fetus on the front porch.

"Look at him," Jake said, shaking his head.

Ben came to his brother's side. "Help you carry him in?"

"If you would. Thanks. Look at him, Ben. My own son."

"Not long ago, it was also your own brother who was curled-up drunk like that. But I'm still alive, and sober now. If that can happen to me, it can happen to him, too. Just be glad he came home, Jake. He could have spent the night on some saloon floor, lying in spit and sawdust."

Chapter Four

Ben walked at his brother's side down Center Street, listening to Jake expound upon life and growth in Ferguson, Colorado, and noticing too the number of glances and reactions Jake received from those they passed Impressive. The surest test of a man's importance, Ben knew, lay in how people reacted to him, and judging from what he saw here, Jake Woolard enjoyed a wealth of influence in this town.

"There are two routes to success here," Jake was saying. "The first and most fundamental is mining. It's the heart and soul of this town. Without it there would be no Ferguson. Nor would there be commerce, and that, by the way, is the second of the two routes."

"Commerce."

"Yes. Supply and demand and all that. Fulfillment, for your own profit, of another man's requisites for making a profit of his own."

"In other words, if a miner needs a shovel and a miner's candle, sell it to him."

"Right. Or, more applicable to what I have in mind for

you on the immediate level: If a man needs a place to sleep in a new town, sell *that* to him.''

Ben looked at a building looming up ahead of them. ''I have a suspicion that I'm about to become the headmaster of the Ferguson sleeping academy.''

Jake laughed. ''And so you are . . . if you'll have it. And only temporarily.''

They reached the big Cathedral of Rest warehouse, with walls two stories high but only one vast room inside, with its rows of curtained windows just above head level. A man inside could look out, but one on the street couldn't look in. ''Clever idea, Jake,'' Ben said. ''Not quite a hotel, but better than putting up in an alley or on a billiard parlor floor.''

''Indeed it is. And there's never a shortage of business, and won't be, not as long as this town attracts newcomers. And that's going to be going on for a long time to come.''

Jake pulled a key from his pocket and thrust it into the door. The door swung inward into a great, hollow, shadowed emptiness. The two men stepped inside, and as Ben's eyes quickly adjusted, he saw that the place wasn't really empty at all, but filled with row upon row of double-level bunks. Not a living soul was in the place.

''I figured there'd be somebody in here taking an afternoon snooze,'' Ben said.

''Nope. One of my rules is that the place is empty by eight in the morning, and stays that way until eight at night. No stragglers and loiterers that way. You want to sleep here, you show up when it opens for an evening, and get in line. First come, first served.''

''No weeklong reservations, eh?''

''No. One night at a time, fifty cents a night. No credit or paying in advance.''

''But what if a man has luggage and such? Does he have to take it out come morning and haul it around with him all day?''

''He does . . . unless he wants to rent a lockbox.'' Jake pointed toward a row of padlocked, heavy wooden lockers lining one portion of a wall. Ben smiled and shook his head in admiration.

"Jake, you are indeed a caution. I never knew you had such a nose for making a dollar."

"I've caught the itch, I reckon. Seen the elephant, as they used to say back in the California gold rush days. Maybe it's because I've struggled so for money for so many years that I've took such a passion for making it here, where the opportunity is so good. And I'm doing well, no denying. I make good money with my sleeping house and my stores, too. And there's mining. I don't do any mining myself, but I have stock in several mines."

"I heard. Sally said you grubstake new miners."

"Some, yes. Those I have a good instinct about. I supply the tools and such in advance in return for a bit of stock in whatever productive mine the prospector might find. Some never amount to much, but others have done quite well for me. And I'm ready to grubstake you, Ben . . . if you want me to."

Ben shrugged. "I don't know a thing about mining."

"It's not hard to learn. There's every kind of man in the world digging in these hills—veteran miners, college professors, bookkeepers, preachers . . . every kind of man in the world short of a Chinaman. No Chinamen in Ferguson. No Celestials allowed. It's a town rule, written right in the ordinances."

"Speaking of rules, what would I have to know to run this sleeping parlor of yours?"

"Not much. Payment in advance, no exceptions. No drunks, no exceptions. No food, no gaming, no smoking while in bed, and no talking."

"Strict house."

"It's a sleeping house. That's all. You don't want to sleep, don't come in. Oh, and no women. Not even alone, and certainly not with a man."

"Not even a man's wife?"

"That's right. This is a one-night-at-a-time sleeping facility for single, sober-minded men. And that's all."

"Who's been overseeing it for you before I came?"

"Lately just a string of short-termers. Before that, Andy did the job. But he ended up ignoring the rules, letting people carouse and drink. Joined in with them, in fact. I had to relieve him of the job. Fired my own son, I did."

"Oh."

"It's hard, anymore, dealing with Andy." Jake looked thoughtfully into a corner of the shadowed room, frowning, his mind on the wayward son who even now was sleeping off last night's drunk back at the Woolard house.

"So what do I do if some two-ton Thomas violates a rule and declares he won't be evicted?"

"You work it out any way you can. Level a shotgun at him if you have to. Generally the others in the place will help get rid of any rule-breakers. It's their sleep that gets disturbed, after all."

"Where do I sleep?"

"There." Jake pointed to a curtained-off little section with a single narrow bunk inside. It was the only segregated chamber in the vast warehouse.

"All right. Will this place be full tonight?"

"It's full every night. Or almost so. Four hundred men. Well, Ben, do you want the job? At least until I can get you grubstaked and make a miner out of you?"

Ben looked around. The truth was, he didn't relish the task of supervising four hundred sleeping men a night, playing landlord, nursemaid, and bouncer all at the same time—but he'd come here to turn his life around, to work. He wasn't likely to be offered anything better anytime soon, and he wasn't willing to freeload off his brother like some tramp.

"I'll take the job," he said. "At least until you can find you somebody reliable to take it over for good. I'm beginning to like the notion of mining. It's my best chance to make something good out of myself. But for now, I'm glad to help you out here."

Jake grinned and slapped Ben's shoulder. "Good. You can start now."

"Doing what?"

"Stripping dirty linens and carrying them to the Smithers

Laundry on up the street. Don't let the abundance of laundry signs in this town fool you: Smithers is the only one worth its soap. I've got an account there. Pay it once a month. Laundry and stolen blankets are my biggest expense."

"How do I decide which sheets are dirty?"

"If they look stiff enough to stand up by themselves, they're dirty. Otherwise, leave them be."

Ben leaned over and examined the nearest exposed sheet with a wince of distaste. "Stains don't count, eh?"

"Stains don't count."

Ben grinned. "I appreciate what you're doing for me, Jake."

"Think nothing of it. Glad to do it." He paused. "It seems I'm unable to save my own son from destruction. At the very least I can help my brother."

"Andy will come around," Ben said.

"Maybe. If he lives long enough."

Three nights later, Ben sat quietly in the darkness on his bunk, staring at the thin fabric wall separating him from the main chamber, listening to the cacophony of snores rumbling and echoing through the big warehouse. He smiled, thinking that it was a good thing that Jake's strict house rules didn't forbid snoring as well as talking and card-playing. Otherwise he'd have to evict half his customers.

He rolled over on his side. Who'd have thought he'd wind up here, high in the mountains where air was thin and veins of ore were thick, where wealth was abundant in the land all around but most men were still poor? When he'd left the service of the Union Army at the close of the great conflict, he'd envisioned quite a different future for himself—a wife, good home, houseful of children, maybe a career in law or business. That future had seemed to be shaping itself for a long time, until death intruded and his family left him for the great world beyond earthly life . . . and he was alone, and miserable.

How many times had he struggled with the desire to see

it all end? How many times had the thought of death seemed as sweet and enticing to him as those soft bunks out there surely seemed to the weary men now occuppying them? He couldn't count on two hands the times he had forced himself to cling to life and hope by sheer force of will, by a pure leap of faith that somehow there was something worthwhile remaining in life, even for a man alone.

There were, after all, things worse than the kind of loss he had suffered. Worse ways to have one's life and loved ones taken from him. He'd seen plenty of that in the days he had ridden with Henry Champion, gathering the eyewitness evidence that finally made a gallowsman out of the murdering devil. Horrible times, those. Men murdered before their families, mere boys shot to death for the sins of their fathers, or because Henry Champion was in the mood to see some poor Union-sympathizing lad jerk and fall at the kiss of a pistol ball.

Ben fell into a deep and undreaming slumber that lasted until the first light of morning began spilling through the big warehouse windows. He sat up and glanced at his watch. Ten minutes later, dressed and with his face washed clean in the basin beside the bed, he stepped out from behind the curtain and clanged the wake-up bell. He was greeted with a chorus of groans and muttered curses as a sleeping army stirred awake.

They filed out past him, most of them grumbling and grumpy, others still half asleep on their feet, and the inevitable few bright and eager early-morning types smiling and looking as if being rousted too early from a comfortable bunk was the finest thing that could happen to a man.

The last man in line was a bald fellow in his mid-forties. "Pardon me, sir, but might I have a word with you?" he asked.

A complaint, Ben figured. "What can I do for you?"

"Is your name, by any chance, Woolard?"

"It is."

"Benjamin Woolard, perhaps?"

"Yes. Do I know you?"

"No. But I do know you. Or who you are. I once

38

watched you sit on a witness stand and talk a wicked man onto the gallows. Back in Nashville. I was a guard in that courtroom, sir, and I stood there listening to you, and I want you to know, sir, I admired what you were doing.''

"Well, I . . . I don't know what to say. Thank you.''

"No, sir. Thank *you*. You were a brave man to do what you did. Infiltrating that bunch of bushwhacking murderers, riding with them, gathering the facts to put Henry Champion where he belonged . . . God bless you, sir. If you never do another fine thing in your life, you've already done the work of the saints by ridding this world of Henry Champion.''

"Thank you. Thank you very much. That means a lot to me to hear you say that, Mister . . .''

"Wilkins. Peter R. Wilkins, from Albany, New York.'' He stuck out his hand for a shaking. "Pleased to know you in person, Mr. Woolard.''

"Pleased to know you, too. You're going to mine, I take it?''

"If I can. A man has to take his opportunities when they come.''

"Indeed. Indeed. Good fortune to you, Mr. Wilkins.''

"And to you too, Mr. Woolard, sir.'' He chuckled. "Quite an odd thing, you know, meeting two men who were involved in bringing the demon Champion to his end!''

Two men? Ben was momentarily confused, then realized that Wilkins must have met or seen Jake. "My brother, I suppose you mean.''

"Brother?'' Wilkins laughed heartily. "I'd say not! This fellow is black as the night sky, and has himself a mouthful of gold teeth.''

"Is his name Roanie? Roanie Platt?''

"I do believe so.''

"I know him. But what did he have to do with the Champion business?''

"He was at the hanging. Saw it happen. You remember the company of Negro soldiers they brought in . . .''

"Yes, yes—because of what Champion did at Saltville.

39

I do remember. But I didn't know that Roanie was among them.''

"He was. He and I had quite a good talk about it only last evening. We'd met one another the day of the Champion hanging, and he recalled me before I recalled him. Quite a nice man. Those teeth are a sight, eh?''

"They are. Well, sir! Thank you for telling me about Roanie. I'll have to talk it over with him if I run across him again.''

Wilkins put out his hand again. "Good day to you, sir.''

"Good day to you.''

When Wilkins was gone, Ben marveled over the remarkable encounter, and the even more remarkable news about Roanie. The past, it appeared, wasn't always as dead as it seemed. It had a way of intruding itself unexpectedly into the present.

He'd almost forgotten that band of black soldiers who had been brought in to see Champion hanged. A deliberately ironic presence theirs had been. Champion, who had murdered wounded black soldiers at Saltville, Virginia, shooting them in their faces without a trace of remorse, had been forced to see black faces staring back at him when his own death came to claim him. A nicely fitting touch, it seemed to Ben.

He locked the door, then made the rounds through the warehouse and checked the sheets. None so dirty as to require laundering, at least not by the standards Jake had laid down. And all the blankets still in place.

He let himself out and locked the door behind him again. The morning was bright and clear, and over at Jake's house, Sally would be cooking one of her excellent breakfasts. He strode into the street and made his way in that direction as fast as he could walk.

Chapter Five

Ben lay awake, hands behind his head, staring at the high sloped ceiling of the Cathedral of Rest and listening to the snores rising from, it seemed, at least half of the bunk occupants on the other side of the curtain.

The noise wasn't what kept Ben awake. He'd been at this job for almost a week now and was accustomed to the nightly serenade of snores. Something else was bothering him, and he couldn't quite pin down what it was. A sense of brewing trouble, as yet undefined.

He was finally about to drift away into slumber when he heard a man's voice, talking in a rough and far too loud whisper, somewhere out in the Cathedral of Rest.

"Come on, you! Show yourself! You ain't fooling me!"

Drunk, obviously. Ben could tell from the slurred words. So this was it: His first round of trouble in his new job. He'd have to evict this man.

Sighing and rising, he pulled his trousers up over his long-john–clad legs and hitched them. Finger-combing his hair, he pushed aside the curtain and exited into the big, dark chamber.

"Come on! Ain't no use in fighting me—I done seen through your game, yes indeedy!"

He tracked the voice and found it belonged to the very man he'd hoped it wouldn't—a burly, ugly, bearded fellow who surely was a prizefighter or strong-arm man. He'd seemed a touch intoxicated when he passed into the Cathedral of Rest earlier, but not enough to make Ben call him down. Clearly, though, he'd slipped a bottle in and had been continuing to drink after climbing into his bunk. The smell of liquor hung like a cloud around his area.

He was in the top bunk, leaning down over the edge, eyeing from an upside-down position a very small and timid-looking fellow in the bunk below him who, curiously, was sleeping with his hat on. His big paw of an arm extended almost to the little fellow's bedclothing, and it appeared he was trying to grab them and pull them away. Or was it the hat he was going after? Ben couldn't tell.

"What's going on here?" Ben demanded, trying to sound as tough as possible.

The bearded head turned up and gazed at him in the darkness. Ben had brought a lamp with him, and now struck a match to it. Light spilled out in a golden circle, and men sat up in their bunks all around, blinking and squinting. Most had been awake already, disturbed by the voice of the drunk.

"Ain't nothing to do with you," the drunk said. "Just get on back to your place."

"Sorry, friend," Ben replied. "There's rules here, and you just broke one of them. No talking. Now, you going to quiet up, or get out?"

"Get the hell away from me, little man," the drunk said again, and reached down again toward the cringing occupant of the bunk below him.

Ben set the lamp on the floor, grabbed the extended arm, yanked back and down, and tumbled the drunk out of the bunk and onto the floor. Twisting the arm around behind the man, he dropped a knee into the small of his back and pinned him.

Ben glanced around. "A little help here would be appreciated," he said.

No one responded—and the pinned man didn't stay pinned long. With a roar and great heave, he dumped Ben off him onto the floor.

Coming to his feet, the drunk swore and said, "You're going to wish you'd minded your own 'fairs, little man!"

Though the drunk had the advantage of size, Ben had that of speed and sobriety. He managed to avoid the man's stomping foot. A bare foot, but a heavy one that would have hurt terribly had it connected.

"Somebody!" Ben yelled. "Give me some help here!" He came to his feet and gave a quick punch; the drunk took it on the nose and grunted, falling back against one of the bunks.

Cursing and furious, the drunk came at Ben, but this time someone did intervene. A nervous but strong-looking man appeared from a nearby lower bunk and stepped in front of the drunk. "You leave that man be!" he shouted with surprising force.

For some reason, the drunk faltered. He paused, staring with confusion at the interloper. Ben took advantage of the moment to come forward and strike the drunk in the jaw as hard as he could. The man collapsed onto his rump, hard. Stunned, he sat there as others now surrounded him. Too many to be defied.

Ben looked around, grinning feebly. "Thanks."

They got the drunk to his feet and hustled him toward the door. Someone found and gathered the man's belongings, most of them still in the cloth sack he used for luggage, and dumped it out the door after him.

The drunk turned on the dark street—still not an empty street, even at this hour—and pointed waveringly at Ben. "I ain't going to forget you!" he yelled. "And you ain't seen the last of me!"

"Don't you try to come back here again," Ben replied. "You're barred from this place."

The man muttered curses, gathered up his possessions, and vanished down the street, which was mostly dark but lighted here and there by saloons and gambling halls that remained open all night.

As Ben started to turn to go back into the Cathedral of Rest, he happened to glance toward the doorway of one of the nearer saloons. There were men there, attracted by the ruckus generated by the ouster of the drunk.

Ben's eyes locked onto the face of one of the men, dimly visible, but clearly enough seen to bring an expression of shock onto Ben's own face.

He stepped forward, staring . . . and the crowd at the saloon door dispersed and was gone.

"What is it?" someone asked.

"Nothing," Ben replied. "Nothing. Well, I reckon we can go back and get some sleep now."

They all reentered the Cathedral of Rest, closing the door and shutting out the night.

As the men filed out of the building come morning, the altercation of the night before was a subject of lighthearted commentary. The light of day had stripped it of its ominous quality, and Ben found himself a warmly regarded hero.

As the small-framed fellow who had occupied the bunk below the belligerent drunk passed by, Ben reached out and touched a shoulder. "Hold up a minute, if you would. I'd like a word."

The dirty face, thin and gaunt, was suddenly full of fear. A quick nod, and the small fellow stood aside until the others were out.

Ben closed the door and looked closely at the fellow. He slowly reached out and removed the hat. Long auburn hair spilled out around the delicate face.

"How did you know?" she asked.

"Same way that drunk last night did, I reckon. Just something different in the look of a woman, even when she's trying to make herself look like a man."

"Nobody else seemed to notice."

"Maybe they didn't. Maybe they did and didn't want to get you in trouble by saying something about it."

She looked dejected. "I'm sorry. I shouldn't have tried

44

to fool you. But I had to have a place to sleep.''

"I know. That's why I didn't say anything last night when I first noticed.''

"Thank you.''

"But it is against the rules. I can't let you do it again.''

"I know.''

"You have a place you can go?''

She looked solemn, and drifted her gaze away from him. "Yes." And he knew from the way she said it that in fact she didn't. But it wasn't really his affair.

"Well . . . I wish the best for you. Where'd you come from?''

"Oh . . . it doesn't matter.''

"Sorry you had that trouble last night.''

She smiled sadly. Sort of pretty, he noticed, though it was hard to tell through the grime on her face. Put there, he figured, to help disguise her femininity.

"What's your name?" he asked.

"That doesn't matter, either. Good-bye," she said.

"Good-bye.''

When she was gone, Ben made the rounds of the sleeping chamber, checking the linens, removing those that demanded a washing. When he reached the place where she had slept, he paused an extra moment.

Intriguing woman. He wondered who she was, and what her circumstances were.

He started to move on, but noted something peeking out from beneath the blanket. He picked it up. A small leather packet, unmarked, held closed by a leather tie. He paused, wondering if he should look inside for identification.

Probably not. She'd surely note she'd left it, and come back for it. Resisting temptation, he tucked the packet under his arm and continued his rounds. When he was through, he placed the packet in one of the lockers, secured it there, and headed out to meet the day.

Outside, he stopped a moment and stared at the place where, the night before, he had seen the shadowy figure that so startled him. He shook his head slowly. Surely not.

Surely it had been his imagination, or some odd coincidence of similarity.

He stepped into the street and strode away.

"Pardon me, sir."

Ben turned. He faced east, toward the rising sun, and had to squint to make out the man who had hailed him. "Howdy."

"Yes. Hello." The man moved to the side, into a more comfortable light. Ben recognized him as one of the men who had helped him evict the drunk. "Sorry to bother you."

"No bother. Thank you, by the way, for the help last night."

"Glad to. Glad to. My name is Hammel. Roscoe Hammel. I've come to Ferguson to mine, like most everybody else, and I've been hoping to find a partner. Well, I figure a man like you, who sees so many folks, might be in a position to know of who else might be looking for somebody to mine with."

"Well, the truth is, I do see a lot of people, but not to get to know them. It's pretty much like you saw it last night: You come in, pay your money, take your bunk, and sleep. No real socializing."

"Right. I see. Well . . . it was just a thought, Mister . . ."

"Woolard. Ben Woolard. Listen, you shouldn't have trouble finding somebody to mine with you in this town, I wouldn't think. The place is crawling with men wanting to mine, and a good number probably need a partner as much as you do. I'll be looking for one myself before long, most likely."

The man brightened with interest. "So you plan to mine?"

"Probably. I'm working the Cathedral right now to help out my brother. He owns the place."

Hammel paused, then said, "Perhaps when the time comes, you might consider me as a possible partner."

Ben was honestly surprised. "I don't really know . . .

what I mean is, you don't really know me. Wouldn't you want to work with someone you knew?''

"Unfortunately, Mr. Woolard, I don't know a soul here. You strike me as the kind of man who can be trusted, and I tend to trust my instincts."

Ben studied Hammel. He had an open and honest face and manner. If instinct was the issue, then Ben's instinct was positive toward Hammel, as Hammel's was toward him. "I'll give it some thought."

"Will I be able to reach you at the Cathedral?"

"There, or through my brother's store. He has the mercantile and mining supply store that stands yonder." He pointed.

Hammel smiled. "Very good. Hope you have a fine day, Mr. Woolard."

"You too, sir."

Late that day, Ben was striding out of the door of a café when he saw Roanie standing at the corner open-air dentist parlor, the smiling dentist at his side, holding a mirror in which Roanie was admiring his brilliantly gleaming mouth. Nodding his satisfaction, he said something to the dentist, placed money in his hand, and turned away, catching sight of Ben as he did. He came over, smiling.

"Covered you over another tooth, eh?" Ben asked.

"Yes, sir," Roanie replied. "That's all of them. Every tooth in my head is gold now."

"What do you reckon your brother will think about that?"

"He'll be jealous, Mr. Woolard. We been racing to see who can get all his teeth golded over first."

"Congratulations on your victory. By the way, Roanie, I met somebody who told me something interesting about you. I hear you were there when the army hung Henry Champion."

Roanie's brows flickered and his bright manner lessened just a little. "Yes. I surely was."

"I was involved in that situation myself."

"Oh?"

"That's right. I testified against him in the trial. I knew some things about his crimes. It was me, I suppose, who was most responsible for putting him on those gallows."

Roanie lifted his head and looked at Ben in a whole new way. "Then, sir, I salute you. Because Henry Champion took something from me. He killed my oldest brother. Murdered him while he lay wounded on a battlefield."

"I'm sorry."

"But I got to see him die for what he done. I watched him hang."

"So did I. You were one of the colored soldiers there, I guess."

"That's right, sir."

"Those were hard days. That bloody war."

"Yes, sir." Roanie paused, running his tongue across his teeth, feeling the smooth gold covering them. "Mr. Woolard, it's funny you should talk about Henry Champion. I was just thinking on him yesterday. Wondering something. Did he have a brother?"

"Champion? No. No. I'm sure he didn't."

"Not disputing you, sir, but I'm feeling sure he did. A twin, matter of fact."

"Henry Champion had no twin brother. No brother at all. I know a lot about the man, and if he'd had a twin, I'd know it."

"But there's got to be a twin, sir. Because I seen him with my own eyes."

"What are you talking about?"

"I seen Henry Champion's twin. Just a few days ago."

"Here? In Ferguson?"

"That's right, sir. Standing inside a saloon, at the bar. I passed it, nighttime, and looked in. And when I saw him, sir, I right nearly died on the spot. Felt a jolting in my heart, and that's the truth. It was like seeing Henry Champion himself again, in the flesh. But older. Like he'd be now, if he hadn't been hung."

"But he *was* hung. He's dead."

"I know."

"I mean . . . I *saw* him hanged."

48

"Yes, sir. Me too."

Ben, more unnerved by this odd tale than he wanted to admit, thought it over. "It has to be a mistake. There is no twin. And Champion himself is dead. So it must be someone who looks like him."

"Just like him, sir. So much like him that it's nigh a miracle if it ain't him. Mr. Woolard? Are you feeling all right, sir?"

Ben was shaken, and apparently it showed. "I'm fine." He forced a smile. Suddenly he didn't want to talk about this matter anymore. "Congratulations on getting your teeth finished up like you wanted."

"Thank you, Mr. Woolard. Did you find your brother?"

"I did. I'm tending his sleeping house for him for now. I'll probably take to mining a little later on."

"All the best to you, sir."

"Thank you."

They went opposite directions. Abruptly, Ben turned. "Hey, Roanie . . ."

Roanie pivoted. "Yes, sir?"

Ben opened his mouth but paused, then did not ask what he had been about to ask, the question that stemmed from the unexpected vision he had seen in that saloon doorway the night before across from the Cathedral of Rest, and which fit all too well, if all too uncomfortably, with what Roanie had just told him.

"Nothing, Roanie. Never mind."

"Good day to you, sir."

"Good day to you."

Chapter Six

Ben knew who had jumped him even before he hit the ground, and chided himself for not having considered the possibility of retribution aimed his way by a man humiliated before an entire warehouseful of others.

He grunted at the impact of the well-trodden alleyway ground against his chest, then yelled when a hard-toed boot caught him in the left ribs.

"Think you can throw *me* out, do you? Think you can make *me* look a fool before four hundred men?" And then the evictee of the prior night kicked him again.

Ben took that blow painfully, but when the laughing attacker drew back and launched a third kick, Ben was ready. His hand shot out, grabbed the man's ankle, and pulled at just the right moment to bring the fellow crashing to his rump.

Ben came up, planning to light into the man while he was down. He hadn't factored in the pain that movement brought to his ribs, however, and that slowed him just enough to allow the big man—who was drunk again, though not quite as drunk as the night before—to rise again and drive a fist into his jaw.

Ben saw stars explode inside his head and staggered back, bumping hard against the side wall of the Cathedral of Rest. He'd been on his way here to open up for this evening's round of sleepers when the drunk had come upon him as if from nowhere.

Stunned and suddenly unable to focus his eyes, Ben groped out blindly and tried to hit his enemy. No connection. The force of his own blow made him stumble out and toward the attacker, leaving him in excellent position to receive the next blow, which caught him on the chin. Consciousness threatening to flee, he went weak in the legs and fell like a puppet with severed strings.

He landed on his knees and somehow managed to stay upright. Putting out his hands blindly to ward off the next blow, he was surprised by a sudden explosion of motion and violence in his swimming field of vision. The drunk cursed and fell; there was thudding and yelling and more cursing . . .

Ben managed to clear his vision enough to see that his attacker had been attacked in turn, and to Ben's surprise, the man who had done it was his own nephew, Andy.

Ben rose weakly and tried to step forward to join the fray. Instead he merely staggered backward, up against the wall again.

"Hey . . . now, wait a minute . . . there . . . that's my nephew you're . . . pounding on. . . ." Ben's voice was breathless and slurred; he sounded intoxicated.

He was also inaccurate about who was pounding on whom. The drunk was doing very little pounding on young Andy, who despite a great disadvantage of size and weight was thoroughly pummeling the man. He fought with a vigor and fury that spoke of pent-up rage and frustration.

Ben opened his mouth to speak again, then swooned and fell to the ground. When he opened his eyes, Andy was looking down at him in the shadowy twilight, an abrasion on his forehead and blood at the corner of his mouth . . . but also a big smile lighting his face. The drunk was gone.

"Ben? You going to be all right?"

"I'm . . . yes . . . I think . . ."

"What the devil did you do to get that man to jump you? He might have killed you if I hadn't been here."

"I was . . . last night . . . threw him . . . out of . . ."

"Come on, Ben. Get up from there and let's get you inside. Wash you up a little and pour a little whiskey down you. Woops! No whiskey for you, I guess. Coffee'll have to do. Come on. I'll help you up."

"Pleased that . . . mighty obliged you . . ."

"Hush. Don't try to talk while you're still addled. Whoooeee! That was a fine time there! I ain't had such fun in Lord only knows!"

"Didn't much think it . . . was fun myself. . . ."

"Hush. Come on." He got Ben to his feet and draped Ben's arm across his own shoulder. Supporting his uncle, he began carefully walking out of the alley, around to the front of the Cathedral of Rest. Ben more or less hung on, shuffling his feet and managing to walk, and wishing his head would quit ringing so loudly.

"I was waiting for you to show up," Andy said, dabbing at Ben's abraded and bloodied chin with a damp cloth. They were inside Ben's little curtained-off chamber, the exterior door closed and locked behind them to keep out customers just yet. "Wanted to talk to you about something. Good thing, huh? I knew there was some kind of trouble soon as I heard that ruckus commence in the alley. Word of caution to you: Don't walk in the alleys in Ferguson at night without looking for somebody to jump you. Half the time somebody will."

Ben's head still hurt but wasn't ringing anymore. He was able to think again, too. "I do thank you, Andy. But what was it you wanted to talk to me about?"

Andy's cheerfulness diminished noticeably, but he retained an open and friendly manner that Ben was only just now beginning to comprehend as quite a significant change from his usual past demeanor. "I wanted to tell you, first off, that I'm . . . sorry. It ain't easy for me to say, but I do mean it. I've been mighty rude to you since you came to Ferguson. I shouldn't have been."

Ben was so stunned, he almost felt he'd been hit again. "Well, I forgive you, then. And I know, by the way, that you've had good reason to feel bitter and sad."

Andy glanced at Ben, then drifted his gaze floorward. "They told you what happened?"

"Yes. And it was an accident, Andy, nothing you need to feel responsible for. It wasn't any more your fault that she died than it was mine that my own family died. It took me a while to see that, though. Sometimes I still feel guilty for it."

Andy looked at him. "It was awful, knowing it was my gun that killed her. I didn't even know it was loaded."

"Forget about it. Forgive yourself and go on. All you can do."

Andy remained quiet for several moments.

"Andy, let me ask you. What made you decide to come apologizing all at once?"

"I don't know, really. Just came around to it, I reckon. I got to thinking about myself, what I was doing, and about you, and how you'd done the same kind of thing after your own tragedies . . . and all at once I knew I was jealous of you. You'd survived. Made it through alive. I was talking every day about destroying myself, but down inside, I didn't want to. I wanted to live again. Like you are."

"I'm not quite living yet," Ben said. "I mean, I'm forty years old, well on through my life, and I've got nothing but a job handed to me by my brother."

"Maybe you can have more."

"What do you mean?"

"It's the other thing I wanted to talk to you about. You interested, maybe, in doing some prospecting?"

"Matter of fact, I am. You?"

"Been thinking about it last day or two. Thinking maybe you and me might do it together."

"Partners?"

"Yep. If you want to."

"Sounds right good to me."

Andy grinned; he was more like the boy Ben had known years back than he'd been since Ben had arrived at Ferguson. "Good. You know, the best way would be to have a third man, too. It's easier with three."

"Well, there was a man who stayed here last night who expressed an interest in finding a partner. I don't know him beyond one conversation, but he seemed a likely enough fellow."

"What's his name?"

Ben searched his mind. "Roscoe Hammel."

"Strong-looking man?"

"Yes."

"Well, heck . . . fine with me, I guess."

"If I see him, I'll talk to him."

"So you really want to do it?"

"Your father's been talking to me about grubstaking me since I came. He just hasn't been wanting to push too hard about it, as best I can tell. But yes, I really want to do it. On one condition."

"What?"

"You do what I've done and give up the drinking."

Andy thought about it and nodded. "I will. I will before I get so lost in the stuff that I can't."

"Wise young man, you are. Proud to claim you for a nephew."

"I am sorry about how I've been."

"You know who you really need to say that to, don't you?"

"Yes. My mother."

"Right. She worries half to death over you."

Andy nodded, then thought seriously, in silence, for several moments. "Ben, does me wanting to change my ways mean that I've given up caring for my lady like I did? Am I forgetting her?"

"You're forgetting the tragedy a little, maybe. Not forgetting her. You'll never forget her. But you have to understand that punishing yourself for an accident does nothing, *nothing,* for the one you've lost. All it does is hurt you and all those who care about you."

"I'll never get over what happened. Not all the way."

"That's true."

55

Andy chuckled all at once, happiness bursting in from somewhere, making him thrust out his hand for Ben to shake. Ben did shake it, firmly, and knew from the light in his nephew's eyes and the joy behind the wide grin that the lad had turned a corner and was on his way to better things.

"Ben, I'm glad to be your partner. When can we get started?"

"Tell you what. Let's talk to your daddy tonight and see when he can get us grubstaked. But let me warn you about something: You've taken on a partner who don't know a blessed thing about mining nor mining law. I can dig a hole and shove a cart, but when it comes to the rules . . ."

"Don't worry. I know most of that already, and Pa can guide us through the rest."

Someone rattled the door; customers for the night were already beginning to gather.

"Well, best open up," Ben said.

"Want me to stay with you tonight, you having took such a pounding?"

"No need. I believe I'll make it. Do I look a sight?"

"Like you've wrestled a pit saw and lost."

"That bad, huh?"

"That bad. . . . Come on. Let me stay. I can take care of everything for you tonight, and sleep out in one of the bunks. You can stay back here behind the curtain and not have everybody wondering what bear you went three rounds with."

"Fair enough. I'll owe you one."

Andy grinned and nodded. "I'll go open the door."

The next two days were filled with activity. At the Jake Woolard household, all was joy. The prodigal had returned! Andy was himself again! Furthermore, he and Ben were going to be partners, mining together, and with Jake naturally sharing some ownership as the provider of the grubstake, it would be a true family venture. Roscoe Hammel, whom Ben found on the street the very day after the initial conversation with Andy, and who had gladly accepted

Ben's offer, would be the only involved party not a part of the Woolard clan.

In the meantime, an event happened that generated much interest in Ferguson. The town's first newspaper opened. No warning or prior ceremony, just a cleanly printed first edition hitting the streets, being hawked by paper-waving, loudly shouting boys in classic style.

Owned and published by a trio of local businessmen who had been victimized in one way or another by crime in Ferguson, the *Ferguson Law & Justice* declared its central theme and purpose in its very title, then spelled it out in full in a lengthy and scathing editorial published just beneath the nameplate.

Ferguson, the newspaper declared quite accurately, was even yet, and to its shame, an oversize mining camp as opposed to a true town of civilized men. The problem: a lack of proper and dedicated law enforcement. The town sheriff, professed the newspaper, was little more than a figurehead, an idle and incompetent symbol who held no true authority, and even worse, no true interest in maintaining law. No wonder men and women were robbed in alleyways by footpads! No wonder prostitution and lewdness thrived in the gambling dens, the upper rooms of the saloons, and on the stages of the theaters! It was time for a new and vigorous assertion of civilization in the high mountains, asserted the *Law & Justice*. Time for Ferguson to rid itself in orderly fashion of the present joke of a town marshal and appoint an authentic and effective replacement, creating a law-enforcement agency well-staffed with tough and fearless deputies who could keep the roughs and rowdies in their places.

Ben, like most everyone else, read the newspaper with great interest. He discussed the matter of the town marshal with Jake, who agreed heartily with the newspaper's sentiments. "The problem with a place like Ferguson is that you get all types, from all over," he expounded to Ben, Roscoe Hammel, and Andy over cigars after a satisfying supper. Sally, filled with a new joy of life, was cooking fine, fine meals now that Andy had declared himself reformed. "There's no sense of permanence and 'home' about a new town. Men come here planning to make a quick fortune, and they think of little else. As long as the rowdies bother the other man and not them, all is fine.

"And rowdies we have, with more coming every day. The lack of good law is like a lure to bad men. They'll swarm to a lawless place like flies to bad meat. I daresay that one out of every ten faces you see on Center Street on a busy day belongs to some man who has reason, beyond the desire for wealth, for forsaking the civilized lowlands for the uncivilized mountains."

"I can vouch for that," Andy threw in. "In the circles I've run in lately, there's plenty of old dark secrets crawling around in the shadows of a lot of men's lives."

"So what will happen?" Ben asked. "Will there be a new town marshal named?"

"Eventually," Jake said. "Having a newspaper to push for it will help a lot. Make people think, you see. Give them a corporate point of reference in addition to their own individualized ones. A newspaper is just the thing to make a town feel like a town, not just a hodgepodge."

"I hope you're right," Ben said, thinking about the attack he had suffered in the alley, and how badly it might have gone for him had Andy not shown up. "I just wonder how bad things will have to get before folks really decide to do something about it."

"Some people getting murdered, most likely," Roscoe said. "I've noticed it always takes people getting killed before folks will get stirred up to fix things."

"You, sir, are a prophet and a philosopher," Jake said, drawing placidly on his long cigar. "Yes, sir, a prophet and a philosopher."

Roscoe looked very pleased. "Really? Thank you, sir. I don't hear that kind of thing much. Most people I know tell me I'm stupid."

Chapter Seven

Andy Woolard held a tack between his teeth and another between thumb and forefinger, the latter being gently but firmly embedded in the trunk of a tree. That one in place, he nailed in the second one as well, then stepped back to examine the document he'd posted on the trunk. A quick nod revealed his satisfaction, and he turned to Ben and Roscoe with a manner much like that of a lecturing professor. The high and beautiful Colorado mountains spread out behind him; before him in the distance lay the smoke-belching, brown and yellow town of Ferguson.

"There, now," he explained. "We've officially posted our notice of claim upon this spot. Later I'll also peel off some bark and etch the same claim right into the wood of the tree, then let the sap run over it and glaze it in to stay. Nobody can swipe off a claim notice that way, you see."

"Now, how big a plot we claiming?"

"Three hundred feet wide, fifteen hundred feet long," Andy said. "That's the law. We'll mark off the rough boundaries in just a few minutes. Now, after we do some digging, and if things then look promising here, we'll bring in a surveyor and get our boundaries clearly defined and registered.''

Roscoe shook his head. ''I don't need a surveyor to know that we're already overlapping another claim. There was due notice posted on a tree, just like you've done, and yonder is one of the boundary markers already in place. And look there—he's done some digging right yonder, already. How can we just run over another man's claim like that, with him having worked it and duly marked it as his?''

Andy whistled between his teeth. Roscoe Hammel was set on obtaining wealth as a miner, but he surely already possessed a wealth of ignorance about how Colorado silver prospecting functioned.

Ben answered before Andy could speak. ''Have you heard of 'surveying in,' Roscoe?''

''No.''

''Well, I'm far from an expert, and Andy can correct me if I'm wrong, but what it amounts to is that it don't matter if our claim overlaps some other fellow's, or his overlaps us. The issue is who makes the first strike.''

''That's right,'' Andy said. ''What'll happen is this: We'll dig around in this land here, just like our neighbor's already done. Then, if we strike silver first, we gain the right to our whole claim, including even the parts of it that overlap his claim—unless, of course, he strikes on his claim first, and then he has the right to any part of his that includes part of ours.''

''I don't understand,'' Roscoe said.

''It's just this simple,'' Ben contributed. ''What counts is who strikes first. You have a successful claim, you get all the claim, and nobody can come along and take part of it from you just because their *unsuccessful* claim happens to overlap your *successful* one. See? That means that even if we encroach on our neighbor there, we aren't really taking anything of value from him. If he gets lucky and finds silver, then that claim is his, and there's nothing we can do to take it from him. Our boundary cuts off where his begins, if he strikes before we do. Same for us if *we* strike first.''

Roscoe shook his head and looked sad. Nice fellow, Ben thought, but surely dumb as a rock.

"Never mind," Andy said. "Don't worry about it. Me and Ben understand it, so you don't have to. All you have to do is dig."

"Well, explain that to me, too," Roscoe said. "Just how does a man go about actually running a mine?"

Andy drew in a deep breath and searched for the simplest way to explain. "All right. First thing is you bring in your tools. Picks and shovels and such. Most haul them in on the back of a mule or two or three donkeys. You pick a spot and you commence to sink a shaft. Down you go, deeper and deeper, putting in timber to keep it braced as you go on down, hauling up dirt and rock with a windlass. You might go deep as a hundred feet or more and find nothing. Sometimes you strike right below the top of the ground. Anyhow, say you've gone down a hundred feet or so, and you've been lucky not to get flooded with water, and you finally hit your contact."

"What's 'contact'?" Roscoe asked.

"It marks off where the barren rock ends and the mineral-bearing rock begins. Well, if you can tell you've hit ore, or are about to, you put up a gallows atop the shaft."

Anticipating the inevitable query, Ben said, "A gallows is what the miners call the timber framework they build over the shafts to put their pullies and buckets and such."

"Right," Andy continued. "Once you get your gallows in, that's where the mule does his work. You tie your rope to him, run it through the pulley on the gallows, and tie the other to your bucket that drops down into the hole. Digging below, you fill the bucket and the mule takes a little walk, pulling up the bucket as he moves away from the shaft. You understand? We saw a mule doing just that while we were coming here."

Roscoe remembered, and smiled, nodding.

"All right. Now say you're doing good and you're going to keep on digging, expanding your mine. You'll probably want to put in a whim at some point. That's kind of a drum that your bucket rope can wind around. The mule turns the drum and winds the rope. Better than the other way, you see. More stable and powerful, and works without the mule having to walk to all creation, back and forth. And once you hit ore that assays out at a hundred or so ounces a ton, you build a shelter house over the shaft.''

"Does the shaft just keep going straight down forever?''

"Of course not. When you hit your mineral, which generally is a hundred or more feet down, you begin running drifts.''

"That's tunnels that run to the side instead of straight down,'' Ben presented. He'd been doing his research for the last little while and was proud to show up smarter than Roscoe . . . not that being smarter than Roscoe was a hard hurdle to leap, he was beginning to notice.

"Right again, Ben. The drifts run out from the bottom of the shaft, and you keep them shored up all along with lagging. That just means posts and lintels, put there to hold back cave-ins. You work on out the drift, and the end of it, where the digging goes on, that's called the breast of the drift. You use tallow candles for lighting, and put in timbers every four feet.''

Roscoe nodded. "That's all I need to know for now.''

Ben and Andy shared a private glance of amusement. *All* he could comprehend for now was probably more the truth.

"Well, gentlemen,'' Andy said, looking from one to the other. "We've posted our claim, we've got our grubstake, and it's a pretty day. What do you say we begin scouting about to figure where to begin digging our hole?''

The Ben Woolard who headed back late in the day toward Ferguson and the Cathedral of Rest was a weary, filthy, and aching version of his former self. He was beginning to have doubts about his fitness as a miner.

He hadn't worked so hard in years, and when it was done there hardly seemed to be more than a dent in the landscape. Thoughts of shafts sinking a hundred feet, even two hundred or three hundred feet. . . . It was more than he could bear to think about just now.

Roscoe had done much better. With the explanations and thinking portions of the business behind, he had fallen to the labor with enthusiasm, working so hard and so enthusiastically, and with such remarkable strength, that Andy had privately joked to Ben that maybe they had wasted part of their grubstake in buying the mule. Roscoe could probably do the work of a mule all by himself.

When the work had begun, Ben was unhappy with the fact that he would have to cease labor earlier than the other two in order to return to the Cathedral of Rest. Jake, unable to find a reliable replacement for Ben at the sleeping warehouse, had begged him to continue his nighttime duties there for a while longer. Ben agreed, on condition that Jake try as hard as possible to find a permanent replacement so that Ben couldn't be accused of leaving his partners to bear more than their share of the mining load.

He didn't feel quite the same now, with muscles throbbing and weariness draining him. He was grateful for the excuse to leave, and the thought of his comfortable bunk enticed deliciously. Striding toward the town, he wondered if he would ever adjust to the physical demands of being a miner.

A stream trickled down from the high peaks. Ben paused, knelt to drink, then looked down at his filthy body. He could hardly crawl into his bed in this state. Looking around, he assured himself he was alone, then stripped down and began to wash, letting the cool water bathe away his aches along with the grime.

Finishing, he let the breeze dry him, then put on his clothes again. Not very pleasant; they were as dirty as he had been. Clearly he'd have to buy himself some extra changes of clothing if he wanted to maintain a modicum of cleanliness.

Motion caught his eye. He looked across the stream and saw a rider descending toward the creek from the nearest ridge. Concentrating on the trail, the man hadn't looked up, hadn't noticed Ben—and when Ben caught a semi-profile glimpse of the face, he was glad of it.

Darting to a nearby grove of trees, he sank to the earth

and watched the rider draw near. He obtained an even clearer view of the face now, and was chilled.

God in heaven, it was true. The man he was watching was none other than Arthur Rellon. Much older-looking than he had been those years before when he rode as the right-hand man and chief assassin for the bushwhacker Henry Champion, but the same man, sure as the world.

Arthur Rellon, a ghost from a dark past, alive and right here in Ferguson! It was enough to make Ben feel sick to his stomach.

He watched as Rellon dismounted at the stream and knelt to drink. Rellon looked about as he cupped water to his mouth, studying the landscape just as Ben had seen him do a thousand times before in the war-torn backcountry of Tennessee and Kentucky. The same small, animal eyes, keen and discerning; the same foxlike cunning in the expression of his narrow face.

Ben hated to admit it, but he had always been afraid of Art Rellon back in his days with Champion. More afraid of him than of Henry Champion himself. Champion killed without mercy, but usually not without at least a perceived reason. Art Rellon killed because he liked it.

It seemed to take an eternity for Rellon to finish his drink and mount up again. He rode on, heading west, vanishing over the next rise.

Ben stood, shaken. Arthur Rellon. It couldn't be . . . but it was.

He recalled the figure he had seen in the doorway of the saloon near the Cathedral of Rest. Jim Masker, or so it had appeared . . . another of Champion's band of wartime murderers. And then there was that wild claim of Roanie Platt, that he'd seen a man who seemed the image of Henry Champion himself.

It was nightmarish. And impossible. Henry Champion was dead. Art Rellon and Jim Masker and all his other agents of death were surely now either dead themselves, or scattered to the corners of the nation. They couldn't be here. It was too much to believe. And Champion, being a dead man, couldn't be anywhere but hell itself, the hell he had richly earned in his foul and wicked life.

Ben headed back to Ferguson, feeling as if the dimming twilight descending upon him was fraught with unseen dangers, full of ghosts.

He reached the Cathedral of Rest and opened it hurridly, eager to get inside and out of the night.

She showed up an hour later. Still wearing her man's garb, still with a face begrimed in a nearly successful effort to feign the darkening effect of a man's whiskers.

He smiled at her. "I knew I'd see you eventually," he said. "I found your packet after you left. It's locked safely away. I'll get it for you."

She smiled, seeming both relieved and uncomfortable. He brought her the packet, which she took and pulled close to herself.

"Thank you," she whispered. Whispered, Ben figured, because if she could pass herself off as a man in appearance, at least to those who didn't bother to look closely, she certainly couldn't alter the femininity of her voice. She turned to the door and began to walk slowly toward it, clearly not eager to go back onto the street.

"Wait," Ben said.

She turned, looking puzzled, almost scared.

"Step in here a moment."

She looked shocked now.

"No, no. It's not what you're thinking. I want to have a private word with you, that's all."

Reluctant, clearly nervous, she came into the chamber. He drew the curtain closed.

"May I ask you again what your name is?"

She hesitated, then whispered, "Deborah Bray."

"Hello, Miz Bray. My name is Benjamin Woolard. Don't worry . . . I'm not going to give it away to anyone that you're a woman. But I do have some concern about you. Do you have a place to stay?"

Her eyes, he thought, moistened slightly in the pause that followed. "No."

"I thought not. You been on the street at night?"

"Yes." She nodded, her eyes very wet now, and her voice growing bitter. "Day and night."

"It's not good, you know, a woman being on her own that way. What I mean is, it's dangerous for you. There's bad men in a town like this."

"I know." She paused. "There are bad men other places too."

"Men—or maybe just one man—that you're running from?"

"Maybe."

"Listen, I don't mean to pry into your private business, but do you mind telling me how old you are?"

"Twenty-five."

She was beginning to speak more readily, beginning to trust him. "Twenty-five. A twenty-five-year-old woman, roaming about unprotected in a dangerous town, hiding, trying to pass herself off as a man. It won't do."

"I have no choice."

He rubbed his chin, thinking. "Do you have a place to sleep tonight?"

"No."

"You do now. You can stay here."

"Out there?" She waved a shaky hand toward the curtain, indicating the building beyond.

"No. In here."

Her eyes, and the way she backed off from him, told him how she took that. He spoke quickly. "No! No! Don't think I'm suggesting anything like what you might be thinking. I'm talking about you sleeping in here, and me sleeping out there."

She frowned. "Why are you being so kind to me?"

"Why shouldn't I be?"

"I just don't understand."

"Look, Miz Bray, I'm just trying to befriend someone who needs it. I can't in good conscience ask a woman to leave a place of safety for the streets, not when I can do something about it."

"But the rules . . ."

66

"I don't intend to advertise any of this. If you don't either, then there's no problem."

She staggered. Without warning. Her face paled. He reached out and steadied her.

"I'm sorry," she said, embarrassed.

"How long since you had anything to eat?"

"I don't remember. A day or two."

"Sit down," he said, waving toward his bunk. "I'm going to get you some food. You stay put until I get back."

"Thank you, Mr. Woolard."

"Glad to help. Now, sit down."

He didn't know what Jake would think about him deserting his assigned place, but Jake wasn't here, and he suspected that if he was, he'd do exactly the same thing. Ben left the building and headed for the nearest café. When he returned, bearing food, he found her asleep on the bunk. Awakening her gently, he gave her the victuals and left her alone in the chamber, going out into the big main chamber and claiming one of the unused bunks.

He lay awake only a few minutes, weary as he was from his day of digging. When he fell asleep, he was thinking of her, wondering just who she was, and who it was she was running from, and why.

Chapter Eight

That night in the Cathedral of Rest, a man screamed out in the darkness, a terrible scream as if hell had risen to claim him. Every soul in the building awakened and sat up, and Ben came to his feet, lit a lamp, and went to the screamer's bedside.

He found the fellow, a mid-fortyish man with a bald head and stooped shoulders, weeping in his bunk, aware now that he had merely dreamed and feeling ashamed of his screaming . . . yet also still very shaken by whatever vision he had experienced.

"It's all right, friend," Ben said soothingly. "Just a nightmare. Nothing more."

"I know . . . I'm sorry."

Ben took a guess. "The war?"

The man looked at him through red and swollen eyes. "Yes. Shiloh."

"Ah, yes. You were there?"

"Yes. I was. And when I dream about it . . . God, it's like I still am."

"No talking!" someone across the warehouse shouted

grumpily, reminding Ben of the house rule. Ben ignored it. As overseer of the place, he could break the rules if there was reason—and calming this man down enough to let him sleep again seemed reason enough to him.

"I wasn't at Shiloh, friend, but I was in the war. I saw things I wish I could forget. When I start to remember them and dwell on them, I have to remind myself that them days are gone. Them situations are past. And all the horrors of it, they're dead and gone."

"I know," the man said. "But sometimes the horrors are like ghosts. Sometimes they rise again. Sometimes they come back."

Ben had no reply. Something in those words shook him. He backed away, frowning.

"Good night, friend," he said. "Try not to dream anymore."

"Good night," the man replied.

Ben took his lamp and headed back toward the bunk, glancing at the curtain that separated his usual sleeping place from the rest of the building. He saw the curtain move and knew she had peered out. He wondered again just who Deborah Bray was, and why she roamed the streets of a mining town dressed as a man and hiding from something, or someone.

He blew out his lamp and lay down. *Sometimes they rise again. Sometimes they come back.* He hoped not. God in heaven, he truly hoped not.

He awakened sometime later in the night, having heard a thudding or bumping sound. He sat up and looked around. Nothing out of place he could see.

Lying back down, he closed his eyes and dreamed about Arthur Rellon, kneeling at a mountain stream and drinking from his hand. The water that streamed through his cupped fingers was as red as blood.

She was gone when morning came. Ben stared at the empty bunk and realized that the bumping he had heard was the thud of the door as she let herself out.

He was surprisingly disappointed that she was gone. Of

70

the mysteries this community was beginning to throw his way, she was the most enticing.

He wondered if she was pretty. Hard to tell, given the man's hat, the hidden hair, the smudged face. If he had to bet, though, he'd bet that she was indeed a beauty. A man could just kind of feel it, even when it was hidden.

He hoped he'd see her again.

Ben, along with Andy and Roscoe, took supper that evening at Jake's house, Ben hurrying through the meal a little to make sure he would make it to the Cathedral of Rest in time to get the doors open at the usual hour.

They talked about mining, of the progress of the shaft, of whether any clear sign had yet been found to indicate good diggings instead of bad. None had. But Andy declared he had a feeling. . . .

Mostly, though, they talked about the big news item of the day in Ferguson. Jake was much more informed about it than the others, having been in town all day instead of out digging in a mine as they had been. Besides, the *Law & Justice* had come out with a special edition that afternoon, full of all the details, and virtually chortling with delight as it reported the abrupt resignation of the town marshal. Jake was the only one of the men at the table who had had time to read the edition.

"The newspaper, as you might guess, hints pretty strongly that it deserves all the credit for bringing the man down," Jake said over a cup of after-dinner coffee, while the smoke of his cigar rose around his fingers. "And no doubt they played a big part. From the way it's reported, it appears he didn't submit a formal resignation letter. It was more or less just: I quit. He declared that the criticism of him isn't justified, that he's done the best job he could, and that the main reason he's quitting is that he hasn't had the mining success he hoped for, and wants to move on somewhere else." Jake puffed his cigar. "But the talk among the merchantry is that there's more to the resignation than that."

"What do you mean?" Andy asked.

71

"The word is that the marshal is scared. Says there's some 'elements' around Ferguson that he doesn't want to deal with, and that are more dangerous than anyone can know."

"I wonder what that means," Ben said. He was thinking solemnly about Arthur Rellon at a stream side, Jim Masker in a saloon doorway, Roanie Platt talking about a man somewhere around Ferguson who looked for all the world like Henry Champion, and about ghosts that sometimes rise again, sometimes come back.

"I don't know," Jake replied. "He could mean any number of things. A mining town always attracts some undesirables. Bold and brazen ones, too."

"Maybe the marshal just didn't have no backbone," Roscoe suggested.

"Maybe."

Andy asked, "So what happens now? Ferguson has no law at all?"

"Not right at the moment. There'll be a new marshal appointed by the town council very soon. The newspaper is editorializing for one who is tough and experienced and ready to hire deputies who are the same. And it's asking the town council to vote in a decent budget for law enforcement . . . and I believe the council is ready to go along with that."

"Any specific potential new marshals named?" Ben asked.

"I've heard a name or two, no one that I know. The one who seems to have the strongest lead, as I hear it, is a man named Jimmy Fraley. He seems to have been doing some self-promotion among the councilmen, and it must be working."

"Hope he'll be a good one."

"Me, too. This town needs to get a strong grip on law and order. Otherwise the wrong elements get too strong, until it's virtually impossible to cast them out. Now's the time for the right kind of citizens to make their claim on this town."

Ben stood. "Well, folks, got to go. Time to open the Cathedral. Sally, the food was delicious."

"I made the pie," Judith chimed in.

"And good pie it was, young lady," Ben said. "Best I've tasted. Well, good night, everybody."

In almost perfect unison they all said their good-nights in return. Ben headed out the door and headed toward the sleeping warehouse, glancing down the street as he neared it.

A town with no law. Not a permanent state, apparently, but certainly the state at the moment. It was frightening, considering what could happen in a town like that. If there was trouble here tonight, for instance, there was no one he could call upon for help.

He hoped the council got that new marshal in place promptly, and that he hired himself a strong force of deputies.

Soon. Before anything really bad happened.

Ben was almost asleep in his chamber when he heard whispers and laughter out in the main section. Shaking his head, he got up, hoping that there wouldn't be a problem this time as there was the last, and feeling a bit headmasterish for having to go hush up a group of grown men. Despite the comfort of his bunk and the security of sleeping in a big, strong, closed building, he was beginning to get tired of this job. He wondered if Jake was really trying hard to get a new overseer, or just sort of letting everything slide conveniently along.

He trudged down one of the rows to where three men, out of their bunks, leaned together, looking at something in the hand of one. They were whispering and laughing like little boys doing something naughty.

"Gentlemen, I'm sorry to intrude on you, but you know the rule," Ben said, and as he spoke the one with something in his hand closed that hand and jerked it behind him very quickly. "Once the lights go out, there's to be no one talking. It disturbs the others, you see." Ben did his best to sound like the cordial voice of reason. He didn't fancy a fight with anybody tonight.

"Why, yes indeed," the man with the hidden hand said. "Very sorry, friend. We'll get in bed right now, and keep quiet."

This *was* like being a headmaster. It made Ben feel old and dowdy. "Very well. Hope all of you sleep good."

"Why, thank you. Same to you."

Ben turned his back and trudged back toward his chamber. He could hear them snickering behind him and could envision the derisive glances they threw toward one another. Again, that headmaster sensation. Oh, well. Went with the job, he supposed. Maybe he and his partners would get lucky at the mine tomorrow and strike ore, and he could tell Jake he was through with this task whether Jake had a replacement yet or not.

When Ben and his partners returned from the mine the next evening, they found that again the day had brought big news in their absence.

There was again law in Ferguson. A new marshal had been appointed—as predicted, Jimmy Fraley—and he was busy building a staff of deputies sufficient to ride herd on so busy and growing a town.

There was a palbable sense of general relief among the law-respecting residents of Ferguson. How the law-disrespecting crowd felt didn't matter. Jake, who told the three miners the news, declared himself among the pleased. Though he hadn't yet met this Fraley fellow, those who had seemed impressed with him.

"A man of grit, that's what they say," he reported. "A man of grit. I've heard that identical phrase about Mr. Fraley from three different men this very day."

Ben asked a question that hadn't even occurred to him until now. "Is there a jail in this town?"

"There is, of sorts. Just planks laid flat and nailed together, one atop the other. Makes for a heavy wall that can't be knocked down. But still not a proper jail, and no proper office for the marshal, either. But one is to be built, a jail and marshal's office together. The council voted that in at the same time they voted in Fraley as marshal, and gave him a good budget besides.''

"Well, may he succeed and thrive," Ben said. "I'm just glad to know there's someplace I can go to if there's any big problem at the sleeping house. By the way, Jake, I'm ready to be replaced, anytime.''

"I know. I'm looking. But don't you like having a good place to sleep every night? And how many men get paid for sleeping?''

"I don't get paid for sleeping. I get paid for scolding grown men for talking to each other, and for getting the holy fire beaten out of me in an alley because I booted a fellow out, and for worrying all night long that something will happen to somebody while I'm sleeping, and I'll be held responsible.''

"All right! All right! I get your message. I'll find you a replacement before the week is out.''

"Promise?''

"No . . . but I'll try. I do promise I'll try.''

"Good. By the way, if there is trouble that I had to call the law in on, where does the marshal make his office until a real one's built?''

"The Palace Hotel, two buildings down from my store. You've seen it—it's the only two-storied building in town. First room on the left on the lower floor.''

"Glad to know it. But with any luck I won't have to ever pay call there. With any luck everything will be nice and peaceful until you find me a replacement, and I can be nothing but a full-time miner and work toward repaying you for that grubstake.''

"I'll find you that replacement as quick as I can.'' He glanced at his son. "Andy, now that you've settled yourself down, maybe you'd like to consider going back to your old job and—''

"Nope. Not me. I'm with Ben on that one. Mining is enough of a job by itself. You can find you some desperate fellow to run your sleeping house. There's plenty roaming the street every day who'd love to have the job just to have a place to sleep safe at night. Speaking of that, where will you sleep once you leave the Cathedral, Ben?''

Ben hadn't thought about that. "I don't know. Maybe I'll go from overseeing the Cathedral to being a paying customer.''

"How you going to pay without a job, and until you strike ore?'' Jake asked tellingly.

Ben paused. "I hadn't thought about that, either. Jake . . . maybe there isn't quite the hurry I thought there was to get out of the Cathedral.''

Jake smiled. "Maybe not.''

"Don't worry,'' Roscoe said. "We'll be striking ore any day now.''

"How do you know?''

"I can feel it.''

"Is that right? Well, we'll just see how accurate your feelings are,'' Jake said. "How deep are you now?''

"Fifty feet or so.''

"You've got a lot of digging left to go before you're likely to hit ore, then.''

"I don't know, Pa,'' Andy said. "It's been found just inches down at some places. I'm like Roscoe. I got a feeling myself.''

"Feelings are fine things, but they assay out at zero to the ton. What I want to hear about is ore, real ore, not feelings.''

"Then just keep listening. You'll be hearing about ore real soon.''

"That's just a feeling, I suppose, Andy?''

"Just a feeling. But a strong one.''

Chapter Nine

The next morning, after another night's round of sleepers vacated the Cathedral of Rest, Ben made his usual rounds to gather dirty linens.

He was passing by the spot where he had scolded the trio of talkers the night before last, when a golden gleam beside one of the bunk legs caught his eye. He knelt, examined it, picked it up . . . and had there been anything in his stomach, he might have vomited it up right on the spot.

He stared for several moments, trying to convince himself that there were explanations for this other than what came to mind. But what if? What if?

Pocketing the item, he left the Cathedral in such haste that he didn't even bother to lock the door behind him.

The Palace Hotel did not live up to its grandiose name. Poorly built and ugly, it seemed bigger than it was because of its false front, which leaned out slightly toward the street even as the entire building seemed tilted to the left. Still, this was one of Ferguson's most substantial buildings, and its only two-story structure. Only the Cathedral of Rest was as tall, though it was only one floor tall, its height resulting from its high, barnlike roof.

Ben pushed past a fat man coming out of the double front doors and ignored the man's protest. The first door to the left stood slightly ajar. Ben walked in without knocking, and a man as fat as the first one, but wearing a homemade badge on his vest, turned a mustached face toward the intruder. The room around him was a disarrayed, makeshift, minimal office, with a rolltop desk and a few chairs here and there. The room smelled of stale tobacco smoke and flatulence.

"What do you want?"

"Are you Fraley? The marshal?"

"No. I'm Wilbert Smith. A deputy."

"Is the marshal about?"

"Not just now, no."

"Then you'll have to help me in his place."

"Help you with what?" The deputy suddenly looked suspicious, as if maybe nobody had informed him that doing this job might actually entail having to *help* somebody.

"I think there's been a murder."

"Murder! Who?"

"Maybe of a man named Roanie Platt. Maybe his brother. Billy, I think his name is."

"What, now? There's a murder, but you don't know who?"

"That's right. Listen, let me explain. My name's Woolard. Benjamin Woolard. I oversee the Cathedral of Rest on up Center Street. You know, the big sleeping place with the bunks."

"I know. Somebody been murdered there?"

"No. But I found this beside one of the bunks." He reached into his pocket and pulled out what he had found: a gilded human tooth, seemingly freshly pulled, still brown-stained from blood around the long and deep pronged root.

Smith squinted piggishly at the tooth. "It's gold."

"That's right. I believe it came from the mouth of either Roanie Platt or his brother. Both of them have all their teeth gilded."

The man frowned. "Wait a minute—you talking about them two nigger wagon drivers with the gold mouths?" He laughed. "You think somebody's been murdering our local niggers, do you?"

"I don't see anything to laugh at here. It seems to me that it's worth checking into. Some people in this town would be mean enough to kill a man for the gold on his teeth, especially if he was a Negro, and looked down on . . . by some."

"Listen here, feller, you can't go thinking somebody's murdered just 'cause you found a gold tooth. There's a lot of folks got gold teeth."

"But this one's been pulled out."

"And from that you figure there's been a murder?"

Suddenly Ben started to feel a little foolish. Maybe, as much as he hated to admit it, this porcine deputy had a point. "Well . . . I don't know that anyone's dead, I admit. It just seemed suspicious enough to me that I thought you'd want to look into it."

"Well, let me have that tooth, and hold it for evidence. I'll see if I can find out who it might have come from. But I tell you, I figure that you're going to find them two niggers still alive and kicking—and there's sure no way I'm going to head off assuming a murder when there's no corpse even been found, nor nobody missing."

"How do you know nobody's missing? Have you seen the Platt brothers anytime the last day or so?"

"I ain't looked. But I will now. And you can do the same. And when you see them, come tell me about it and I'll give you this tooth back. Finders keepers, I reckon."

"I don't want the tooth. And I will look for the Platts. And if one or both of them turn up missing, I expect Marshal Fraley will want to find out what's happened."

"Let's just take 'er one step at a time and see. And keep in mind, this ain't as big a thing as it might be, even if there has been a killing. We're just talking about a couple of niggers, after all."

Ben drew in a deep breath, not sure what to say to a

man like this. "I'll let you know if I find out anything," he said.

The deputy grinned, a vague edge of mockery hiding beneath the yellow-toothed smile. "You do that, feller."

Ben glanced back as he left. The deputy was looking into a cracked mirror on the wall, finger hooked under his upper lip, the other hand holding the gold tooth against one of his own, just so he could see what it would look like.

Ben knew there would be no inquiry from the marshal's office about the Platts. And if this man was typical of the kind of deputies the new local law was hiring, he didn't have too high a hope for the future of law enforcement in Ferguson.

If the Platts were to be found, he'd have to do it. But how could he go about it without shirking his duties at the mine? He'd sworn to himself that he would carry his share of the load. He was the oldest of his group, but determined to work as hard as Andy, the youngest.

He'd have to wait to find the Platts, that's all. Maybe the deputy was right. Maybe a gold tooth found by accident didn't really mean much. Maybe he was jumping too far to the conclusion that a gold tooth equaled evidence of murder.

Suddenly hungry for his breakfast, he headed for one of the nearby cafés, from whence the smell of eggs and grease wafted in a thick, almost visible effluvium. Miner's food. Fare for men who would work off whatever they ate and more before their long day finally ended.

Ben ordered ham, coffee, biscuits, potatoes. He ate it all without tasting a bite, thinking about that golden tooth, and keeping an eye toward the window all the time, hoping he'd see either Roanie or Billy pass by outside. He saw neither. After wiping his mouth on the checkered napkin, he paid his bill and left, heading for the mine and trying to put aside thoughts of anything but the job at hand.

They worked hard all day, making their shaft deeper, shoring it with timbers, and beginning to wonder, secretly, if they were going to find any wealth in this place at all.

The Gallowsman

It was easy to dwell on the promise of mining in the days before the work began. Wealth, lying right in the ground, ready to be claimed, ready to transform a man's life . . . it seemed magical and marvelous.

Only when the actual grueling labor came about did the other side present itself. Sure, wealth might be there . . . and equally so, it might not. No, more than equally so: The odds against success were greater than those favoring it. For every man who came to the mountains and became a tycoon, how many were there who lost it all?

Ben had never worked so hard with nothing to show at day's end but a hole that was a little deeper. What if they went down into the depths and found nothing? All this digging, all this framing of timbers, hauling of load upon load of rock . . . In the end there might be nothing to show for it but a dark pit, and the prospect of starting another such pit somewhere else, with equally chancy odds of succeeding.

"Let me ask you boys a question," Roscoe said when they broke at midday to eat the food they'd packed for themselves. "Once a fellow hits him some ore, what happens after that?"

"Well," began Andy, the usual answerer of Roscoe's endless queries, "what happens first is that somebody looks the ore over as it comes up out of the hole. Most likely that'll be me, in that I've been here the longest and have learned a bit more about this business than the rest of you. After time, it may be one of you doing it, if you prove to have a good eye for it. The ordinary ore will go into a pile, or a dump, and that will go in the back of a wagon and get hauled down to one of the smelters in town. That gets sold by the ton.

"The good ore, on the other hand, that'll probably go entirely out of Ferguson. The good stuff is generally bought up by purchasers out of the smelters in Pueblo or Omaha, or maybe even St. Louis. That's sold in hundred-pound quantities, bagged up."

"How do you know the good ore from the bad?"

"Well, like I said, some have an eye for it, can tell from

looking about what an ore is going to assay. But to really know, you've got to have the stuff assayed out in town. If you're really lucky, you can make fine money. I know of one mine that stumbled here recently into some ore assaying out at a thousand ounces of sliver per ton. We'll do the same. I can feel it.''

"Your mouth to God's ear," Ben said.

When the too-short luncheon was finished, it was back to labor again, until finally the hour began to grow late and Ben took his welcome leave to return to Ferguson and Jake's warehouse full of bunks.

He washed again in the stream, but felt very odd and endangered while doing so, thinking that any moment Art Rellon might show up like he had the time before, recognize the miner at the stream as the very man whose testimony sealed Henry Champion's fate on the gallows . . . and then it would be over for Ben Woolard. His blood would stain this stream red, and nobody would ever know who had killed him.

Rellon didn't appear, however, and Ben made it back into town without incident . . .

. . . and saw, to his joy, the distinctive form of Roanie Platt striding down one of the boardwalks, going away from him.

Thank God! Ben felt a joyous wave of relief.

"Roanie!" he called, jogging toward him. "Roanie, wait!"

Roanie turned, but no golden smile beamed this time. He looked at Ben with the strangest expression. "Howdy," he mumbled when Ben came near.

"Roanie, I'm glad to see you. I been worried about you today."

"Worried?"

"Yes. I'd thought . . . well, never mind what I thought. You, uh, ain't lost a tooth by some chance lately, have you?"

"A tooth? Why you asking me about teeth?"

Ben could tell something was weighing heavily on his

black friend. There was no cordiality, no "sir" at the end of every phrase. "What's wrong, Roanie?"

"It's my brother Billy. He's gone. I ain't seen him for three days now, and I can't find nobody knows where he might be."

Ben felt his legs turn to water and his hands begin to tremble. "Roanie . . . there's something I need to tell you."

"Something to do with Billy?"

"Maybe. The reason, you see, that I was worried about you today, and the reason I asked about your teeth, is because of something I found in the Cathedral of Rest. It was a gold tooth. Like yours . . . like Billy's. Pulled out by the root. Somebody had dropped it on the floor."

Roanie drew in a long, trembling breath and stared at Ben a few moments. "Let me see it."

"I can't. I took it to the town marshal's office, asking for him to look into it, to make sure you and Billy were all right. He wasn't there, but a deputy was, and he took the tooth as evidence."

"He going to be trying to find out if it's Billy's?"

"He said he would, but he won't. He . . . didn't seem to think a colored man was worth worrying about."

Roanie was silent again. "Billy's dead," he said at last, very flatly. "Billy's dead, and somebody's pulled out his teeth for the gold on them."

"That's the fear I had. But my first thought was that maybe it was you who was dead. That's because it's you I know, not Billy."

"Murdered. I was afraid of that." Roanie was struggling not to cry.

"You don't know he's murdered, that he's even dead. We don't know that the tooth I found was his at all."

"He's dead, sir. I been feeling it in my heart and my bones all day. He's dead. And I believe I know who killed him, sir."

"Who?"

A pause, then: "Henry Champion, sir."

"Henry Champion is dead, Roanie."

83

"No, sir. He ain't dead. He's alive, and he's here, and he's killed Billy."

"You're not making much sense. How could a dead man be alive?"

"Because he just is, sir. I seen him again. With my own eyes. And he seen me, outside of town it was, and tried to get two of his men onto me, to catch me. He'd have killed me, sir, if they had caught me. For my teeth, I reckon. Or maybe he recollects my face from seeing me in the crowd of nigras who watched the day they hung him. But no. No. He wouldn't remember that. One dark face would look like any other to him." Roanie ducked his head suddenly, and tears came. "I reckon he wanted me just so he could get my teeth. He didn't get me, but he must have got Billy. And now Billy's dead. Dead."

"Roanie, listen. One, we don't know that Billy's dead at all. All we've seen is a gold tooth, and that could have come from anywhere. Two, we *do* know that Henry Champion is dead. We saw him hanged back in '65. Three, I believe I know who had this gold tooth to begin with, and it wasn't Henry Champion. There were some men in the Cathedral, talking after the lights were out. I called them down, made them shut up. One of them had something in his hand he was showing the others. I believe it was this tooth."

"Why would he be showing off a gold tooth unless there was a reason? Unless there was a story to go with it?"

"I don't know. All I'm saying is, don't jump to conclusions. Billy may turn up at any time, alive and well, with every tooth still in his mouth. Then you'll feel silly about all this Henry Champion nonsense."

Roanie was firm. He shook his head. "I respect you, sir, and 'preciate what you're trying to do here. But there's two things I'm sure of, and I'll not be shook from them: My brother Billy is dead, and the man I saw was Henry Champion himself, just as alive as you and me, and right here in Ferguson."

And with that Roanie turned and walked away. Ben

watched him go, then headed for the Cathedral, eager to get inside, into his chamber and his bed, and to pull the curtain across like a child pulling his blankets over his face to hide from the dark ghost in the corner of the nursery.

Chapter Ten

Ben found himself confused when he pulled out his key to unlock the Cathedral door and found it already unlocked. Had Jake come and let himself in for some reason, or had Ben simply neglected to lock the door when he left that morning?

Remembering the state he was in during that departure, he decided the fault was his. Chagrined and hoping that no one had taken advantage of the unlocked door, he poked his head in, looked around, and took a quick tour of the building. Nothing amiss that he could tell. Heading to his own sleeping area, he yanked back the curtain, then leaped backward with a yell of surprise.

The person on his bunk let out a yell, too, and bolted upright. Ben stared into the fear-paled face of a person freshly jolted out of deep slumber.

He let out a slow breath. "Miz Bray, I do believe my heart almost gave out on me just then."

"I'm sorry," she said. "Please, don't be angry at me."

"You shouldn't have come in here with the place not open."

"But the door was unlocked."

"I know. My mistake." He sighed loudly, his heart now slowing to its usual rhythm. "I left in a hurry this morning and failed to lock it behind me."

"It was a godsend for me," she said. "I needed a place to hide."

"Something wrong?"

"Yes. Mr. Woolard . . . I'm in trouble. In danger, I think. I need help. You're the only person in this town I know to turn to."

"What kind of danger?"

"There's someone in town now who might hurt me."

I think I know the feeling, Ben thought wryly. "Who?"

"A man."

There was a stool just outside the curtain. Ben pulled it in and sat down. Deborah Bray, meanwhile, had swung her pantalooned legs down to the floor, and sat facing him with her hands resting on the bed on either side of her. Ben asked, "Your husband?"

"No. I have no husband. It's my brother. My *half* brother, actually."

"Why would your own half brother want to hurt you?"

"Because he's afraid that I might hurt him. And I will, if I can."

"What have you got against him?"

"Nothing but the fact that he murdered my father."

"That's a serious charge. You can prove it?"

"Yes, I think I can." She reached beneath the covers and pulled out the same packet she had left in the Cathedral once before. "With these."

"Papers?"

"Documentation. Copies of letters between my half brother and one of his business associates. Letters that were supposed to be destroyed, but which I managed to save from the fire. They contain communications concerning the planned murder of my father. He'd become wise to some of the thievery and crime my dear brother and his associates had involved themselves in. He was prepared to turn them over to the law. They had to get him out of the way."

"If that packet contains documents as important as all that, why did you let yourself forget it the other day?"

"Because I'm so tired, so hungry, so scared, that sometimes I almost forget who I am." Her voice began to crack with emotion. "I came to Ferguson because I thought I could find the help I needed here from an old friend . . . but he wasn't here. He was supposed to be, but he wasn't. I looked for him for days, disguising myself in case Daniel—that's my half brother, Daniel Bray—came looking for me. Finally I found the man I was looking for. He's buried in the cemetery at the edge of town."

"I'm sorry. A beau?"

"In a way. Some years ago. It doesn't matter now."

"Deborah—may I call you Deborah?—would this brother of yours actually *hurt* you?"

"He'd not only hurt me, he'd kill me. He's a wicked man, Mr. Woolard."

"Ben. My name's Ben. Listen . . . I don't quite know what to do. I'm glad you felt good enough about me to come here, but obviously you can't just keep hiding here forever. We could go to the law . . ."

"I don't trust the law. I've seen the law put into the pocket of too many wicked men to trust it anymore."

"Well, from what I've seen so far of the law in this town, I ain't too impressed myself. There is a new marshal, but I haven't met him. Just one fat deputy."

"I don't want to go to the law. I want to hide until I can get away, and get these papers to . . . someone. I don't know who. Someone who would know what to do, and who would prosecute Daniel for what he did."

Ben rubbed his chin, thinking. "Tell you what. Why don't you stay here another night—I'll sleep out yonder with the rest of them again—and tomorrow I'll take you to my brother's place. His name is Jake Woolard, and he's a good man. He has influence here. He'll have good advice, and his house is big enough that they can keep you safe for a while."

She smiled. "Thank you. Thank you so much. I felt that I could trust you."

The smile answered the question: She *was* pretty. Ben smiled back. "I'll do all I can for you. Tell me. When was your father murdered?"

He wished he hadn't asked that, for any happiness she had shown instantly vanished. "I don't much like talking about it."

"I'm sorry. Well . . . it's time for me to let in the evening's customers. Are you settled back here?"

"I'm fine."

"Had anything to eat lately?"

"No."

"I'll fetch you something in a few minutes, then."

"I have no money. . . ."

"You don't need it. I'll take care of it."

"You're too kind to me, Mr. Woolard . . . Ben."

"Nah. Just trying to be the gentleman my mother raised me to be."

"I'll repay you when I can."

"Forget about it. Now settle in, and let me go out to fetch the food. I'd best do it before I let any customers in, or else my brother would have my head for leaving the place untended with folks inside. He owns this place, you see. In fact, he'd probably have my head for forgetting to lock the door this morning."

"I'll not say a word."

"Thank you. Now stay put, and I'll be back quick as I can."

He strode down the crowd street, lost in thought, feeling a mix of excitement, intrigue, and doubt.

The excitement and intrigue were easily accounted for. What man wouldn't be pleased by having a young and attractive woman coming to him for refuge, seeing him as a source of strength and security in time of danger?

He wasn't sure where the doubt came from. Here was this strange woman, disguised as a man, roaming the streets of a town for days, carrying about a packet of supposedly important papers, and now turning to a virtual stranger for help and telling a wild story of a patricidal half brother roaming about, ready to kill her.... It was a lurid and strange tale, to be sure. One he wasn't sure he could believe.

There was a lot going on, come to think of it, that strained his credulity. All this talk of a hanged man actually being alive, these visions of old enemies popping up like flesh-and-blood ghosts all about... who would have thought it? Even now, Ben wasn't sure what to think about it all.

He reached a café, ordered up a box of bread, beans, and beef, and carried it out into the darkening street. Glancing at his pocket watch, he realized it was after his time to open up the Cathedral. He hoped Jake wouldn't chance to come by and wonder why his brother and employee was failing to do his job in timely fashion.

He quickened his pace, then came to a dead stop.

Directly before him on the boardwalk, staring into his face, was Arthur Rellon.

Ben stood like a statue, looking at Rellon in disbelief, and seeing in Rellon's eyes the rising light of recognition. No words were said, no expressions changed... just mutual stares, mutual recognitions, mutual remembrances of a time long past, when they had ridden together in a bushwhacker's band, and a time shortly afterward when Ben had betrayed that band's leader on the witness stand in a military courtroom.

Ben found himself wanting to speak, yet also wanting to do anything but speak. He wanted to walk on and pretend that he hadn't seen this man, that nothing important had happened here.

But all he could do was stare.

Art Rellon was the first to move. He broke off the gaze and walked on past Ben, his shoulder actually brushing against him. Ben turned and watched him go, and when Rellon was half a block away, he turned as well, and looked back at Ben another long moment.

Ben actually had to fight the impulse to run, and he wasn't by nature an easily frightened man.

When he reached the Cathedral, men were already lined

91

up at the door. He apologized for his lateness, told them to be patient another moment or two and he'd have the door opened for them. He then admitted himself, closing and locking the door in their faces, with further apologies.

She was eager for the food. He didn't think he'd ever seen a human being eat with such vigor. After drawing the curtain and closing her in, he returned to the door, opened it, and began admitting another night's army of soon-to-be sleepers.

He studied the face of each man who entered, fearing that he would see again the face of Rellon, or Masker, or even Henry Champion himself. Henry Champion, the dead man.

Henry Champion, the man Roanie Platt swore wasn't really dead at all.

He saw the curtain move, and glanced that way. She was peering out like a mouse from a hole, watching the men file in. She, too, he knew, was looking for a particular dreaded face.

The last man entered, and Ben closed the door. Another nearly full house.

Ben went to his bed and lay down, looking at the ceiling.

Imagining that he could see Arthur Rellon up there in the darkness, staring down at him like a hanging bat.

He had only just drifted off to sleep when he heard movement near the door. Sitting up, he caught a glimpse of the door opening, shutting, and someone slipping out.

Deborah Bray. Leaving again.

He'd fallen asleep fully dressed except for his boots, and so he rose quickly and darted after her, shoeless. What was this business of leaving on the sneak, after all this talk about danger and needing a place to hide?

She had gone less than a block when he saw her. He ran after her and put his hand on her shoulder. . . .

She wheeled and gave a low, muffled screech, and waved a knife at him, almost nicking his face.

"Be careful!" he snapped. "What are you trying to do—kill me?"

"I'm sorry," she said, her voice very strained. She was taut with fear. "I'm sorry."

"Why are you leaving? I thought you needed a place to stay."

"He's in there, Ben. Daniel came through that door. The last man. I almost died to see him. . . . I waited until everyone seemed to be asleep, and I fled."

"Look, if he's a murderer, then maybe we're just going to have to trust the law after all, and go have a talk with the marshal."

"No! No. I can't." She pulled away from him and turned.

"But what about my brother's house? Tomorrow I was going to take you there, and—"

She ran down the street and was gone.

Ben turned slowly and walked back to the Cathedral.

The devil with her. It was probably all lies or insanity anyway. What sensible woman behaved the way she did?

She'd best not come back, he told himself. She'll get nothing more from me.

Ben watched every man leave the next morning, trying to recall which had been the last to enter the night before. He couldn't recall. Didn't matter anyway. He had enough to deal with without taking on the fantastic concerns of an unstable woman.

Half an hour later, he was on his way to the laundry with another load of dirty linens when he heard a hubbub down the street. It was continuing, and a crowd gathering, when he came out of the laundry again.

He overheard the word *murder*, and something about how awful it was, this business with the teeth. . . .

He joined the crowd, pushing his way through until he was near the front of it.

The fat deputy was there, with another deputy, and a slender, young man who he assumed was the new marshal.

On the ground before them, covered with a sheet but with the face momentarily exposed, was the body of Billy Platt. His mouth was open. All his teeth were gone.

Chapter Eleven

Ben stared. The dead, dark face, eyes partially open, formerly rich-colored flesh now taking on a graying hue . . . and most of all, the jaws wide open, dark holes where teeth had been, flies buzzing in the gaping mouth, crawling upon the wounded and ugly gums.

"What happened?" Ben asked a man beside him.

"They found him hidden in a gully an hour or so ago. Found him by the smell. Stinks, don't he!"

Another man joined the conversation, as strangers will at such times. "What I can't figure is the teeth. I know a lot of men with no teeth in their head, but them gums look like his was fresh-pulled."

The first stranger answered, "Torture, I'll betcha. Lot of old hardshell Confederates and such still roaming this nation, despising your coloreds. Pulled them out to torture him, then killed him. That's what happened."

"At least it didn't happen to a white man," the second stranger said, shuddering.

"It was for the gold," Ben said, feeling and sounding somewhat dazed.

"What?"

"His teeth were gold. They pulled them for the gold."

"You knew this coon?"

"Know his brother."

As if cued in by those words, Roanie Platt appeared at the edge of the crowd and shoved his way through rather roughly. Such behavior from a black man would have been scarcely tolerated at most times, but the crowd quickly clued to the suspicion that the dead man and the newcomer were probably related, and allowed Roanie to shove in without protest.

Roanie stared at his brother's dead form. Just stared, said nothing.

Ben approached him and touched his shoulder. Roanie didn't seem to feel him. "Roanie. I'm sorry."

"It was Champion," Roanie mumbled. "Henry Champion murdered him."

The same old impossible story . . . or was it impossible? There was the matter of having encountered Art Rellon on the boardwalk. Ben scanned the crowd quickly, looking for Rellon's face. He wasn't there.

The young neophyte marshal rose from his position by the corpse and faced Roanie with a frown. "Who are you?"

"My name's Roanie Platt, sir."

"You know this dead nigger?"

"He's my brother . . . sir."

"Your brother, huh? Hey, open that mouth wider."

Roanie complied. The marshal gazed at the golden spectacle, then turned and grinned at his deputies. "You see that? Ain't that just like a nigger, wanting his teeth gilded over!" The smile vanished and he addressed Roanie again. "Why your teeth like that?"

"Just because I want 'em so, sir."

"This dead boy, he have the same thing?"

"Yes, sir."

"Don't it strike you as a bit foolish, running around a town with a mouth full of gold? There's a lot of folks struggling to make their living, struggling to keep food in their bellies until they can make a strike, who'd likely re-sent seeing a common buck nigger running about with his mouth full of gold.''

"I expect so . . . sir.''

"You think it's the job of the law to protect foolish niggers who ain't got the sense to avoid provoking the public?''

"My brother was murdered, sir. I believe it's the job of the law to find who done it, and punish them.''

Ben stepped forward. "Pardon me. My name's Ben Woolard. I run the Cathedral of Rest for my brother, Jake Woolard. I saw something the other night that might be relevant to this, and I already brought it to the attention of one of your deputies.'' He pointed at the fat man. "That one.''

The big deputy gave Ben a hateful look, then turned it to an expression of innocent confusion and shrugged at his superior. "Marshal, I don't know what he's talking about.''

"Yes, you do. The gold tooth I brought you. The one I found on the floor of the Cathedral. The one you kept as evidence.''

"I ain't never seen this man before, Marshal,'' he said. "I swear.''

Marshal Fraley frowned at Ben. "Mister, I'm trying to conduct a proper investigation of a nigger murder here, and would appreciate it if you'd stay out of it.''

"Your deputy's lying to you, Marshal.''

"Step back, sir, and keep your mouth shut.'' Fraley turned back to Roanie. "What'd you say your name was, boy?''

"My name is Roanie Platt. My brother there is . . . was named Billy.''

Fraley glanced at the fat deputy. "Write that down.'' Back to Roanie. "When did you last see your brother?''

"Been some days ago, sir. Right now my mind's all foggy, Marshal, and I can't recall exactly.''

"Can't recall, eh? Can't recall.'' He said it as if it were significant.

Somebody approached Fraley from the crowd and whispered in his ear, with their eyes cut toward Roanie all the while. They withdrew, and the marshal gave Roanie a piercing look. "Tell me, boy, is it true that you and your brother had a little contest going over these teeth, trying to see who could get the most teeth gilded over first?"

"We did, sir. Just a friendly thing."

"Friendly. Friendly. Looks to me like somebody wasn't feeling too friendly toward your brother."

"I know who killed him, sir."

"Do you, now?" At this point, it seemed to Ben, that the professional approach would be to take this rather absurdly progressing interrogation off the street and out of the public eye and ear, but Fraley, despite all the talk of his experience as a peace officer, didn't seem to be as professional as Ben would have expected. He went ahead and asked the question. "Who done it, then?"

Roanie glanced around, caught and held Ben's eye a moment. "Henry Champion, sir."

Fraley cocked his head. "Who?"

"Henry Champion, sir. He murdered Billy. And he tried once to murder me."

"Who the hell's Henry Champion?"

"He was a rebel, sir. A bushwhacker in the middle part of Tennessee and Kentucky during the big war."

"*That* Henry Champion?" Fraley grinned. "Boy, the Henry Champion that bushwhacked in them parts is long dead. He was hung by the neck in '65, best I've heard."

"Yes, sir. I know. I was there to see the hanging."

"But you think this hung man killed your brother?" Fraley laughed. "What's wrong with you, darky? You lost what mind you ever had?"

"Henry Champion ain't dead, sir. I seen him myself, more than once, right here about Ferguson."

"Know what I think, boy?" Fraley said. "I think that what we might have here is a case of two nigger brothers getting all caught up in competing with each other over these fool gold teeth, and when one got ahead of the other, the other got mad, maybe drunk at the time, and murdered the other one over it, and pulled out the teeth for spite."

"I didn't kill Billy, Marshal, sir."

"What I can't figure is why you'd make up such a fool tale to try to cover it. Least you could have done was blame it on somebody who's really alive!"

"I ain't lying, Marshal. I didn't kill Billy. Henry Champion did. And he *is* alive! He is!"

"Come with me, boy. You and me got a lot of talking to do." Fraley nodded to his deputies. "Get this body took care of. Get it off the street before it stinks the whole damn town up. And find us a picture-taker to get some pictures took before we bury him."

Ben stepped forward and took Roanie's arm. "I'll talk to you later."

"Get away from the prisoner, friend!" the fat deputy snapped.

"What'd you do with that gold tooth I brought you?" Ben asked sharply. "You sell it, or gamble it off?"

Fraley intervened. "You keep claiming you had a gold tooth in your possession, and we may be talking to you, too. Now, be on your way. All you folks! Clear out!"

Ben longed to speak, but knew it would be ill-advised. He bit his tongue, gave Roanie a final glance and nod, and turned away, heading on down the street for some fresh air.

Ben worked all day in distraction, hardly able to concentrate. He said nothing about the murder to the others. It had nothing to do with them or anyone they knew . . . and the whole angle involving Champion seemed ridiculous.

And surely it was ridiculous. As he worked with pick, shovel, bucket, and pully, Ben forced himself to pull back from the situation and evaluate it objectively. Obviously Henry Champion was dead. The federal government had made sure of it long ago. Just as obviously, Roanie Platt, who had more reason than most to be sure that Champion was in his grave, was convinced that he had seen none other than that very man. Had even been attacked by him.

The only possible answer was that Roanie had seen someone who looked like Champion. And was that so unreasonable a hypothesis? Champion had been a fairly ordinary-looking fellow. It had been years since Roanie had seen him, and even then he'd only had a view of him from a prison yard, with Champion briefly standing unmasked on a gallows before the trap was sprung. There was no reason to think that Roanie's knowledge of Champion was so intimate that he couldn't easily be mistaken, especially after all these years.

And hadn't Roanie said that Champion had murdered another of his brothers during the war? That was entirely believable—Champion had murdered several wounded black soldiers—and might account for Roanie's readiness to link the idea of another murdered brother with Champion. It was all a mental misfire on Roanie's part, brought on, no doubt, by the stress of worry and hard work.

And what of Ben's own sighting of Art Rellon? Well, it was in fact possible that it was Rellon he'd encountered. Rellon had survived the war; unlike Champion, he'd been neither tried nor hanged. He might well be in Ferguson. Or, again, it might be a coincidence of physical appearance. Someone who looked a bit like Rellon might look after so many years. That look of "recognition" he'd seen on Rellon's face might have instead been a look of concern or surprise at the intense way Ben himself was probably staring at him.

And as for that brief sighting of a man who looked like Jim Masker—hang it all, that had been a nighttime sighting in far from ideal circumstances. It probably wasn't Masker at all. And even if it was, there was nothing inherently inconceivable about the notion of Jim Masker being alive.

By the end of the workday, Ben had substantially convinced himself that the world was a far more reasonable and common kind of place than he had been letting himself think. Henry Champion was dead and gone, Art Rellon and Jim Masker were either absent or irrelevant, and Roanie Platt was operating under illusions to which he, Ben Woolard, would not let himself fall victim.

If there was any dangerous person in and about Ferguson with whom Ben should concern himself, it wasn't Champion or any of his old cohorts. It was Daniel Bray, the threatening brother of the lovely Deborah Bray, a woman who, no matter how unusual, was yet the object of many an increasingly pleasant thought for him.

He worked until it was time to go back to town. Bidding his partners farewell and feeling more at peace with the world than he had for the last little while, Ben strode through the late of the day toward Ferguson, whistling and wondering how things had gone for Roanie.

At the edge of town, Ben paused at the graveyard and noted a freshly filled grave. Billy Platt's probably. He shook his head. Sad, the poor fellow being murdered like that. He only hoped, for Billy's sake, that the tooth-pulling had occurred after death, not before.

He would later think it ironic that he was thinking about that when he spotted the man who had been in the Cathedral, talking and showing something—the gold tooth, Ben presumed—to those other fellows. The man was walking along, much as Ben was, heading back toward town from another of the trails leading down from the higher climes. Ben glared at him, unseen, then on impulse decided to have a talk with the man.

"Hey, there! Friend! Can I have a word?"

The man stopped and watched as Ben trotted toward him. He seemed wary, so Ben put on a smile and a congenial manner.

"Howdy, there. Sorry to bother you. Do you remember me?"

The man frowned at him and shook his head.

"I met you the other night in the Cathedral. The sleeping house."

"Oh." The man looked closer, then remembered. "Yeah. It was you who came over like a schoolmarm and told me to shut it up."

"Sorry about that. House rules, and my brother owns the house. In fact, I'm only working there for him temporarily, until he can find a permanent replacement." He grinned warmly, doing his best to show that he was just a regular old fellow, no schoolmarm after all.

"Yeah. What can I do for you today, then?"

"Well, it happens that I found something over near your bunk sometime after you left, and wondered if it might be yours. A gold tooth."

"You found that, did you?"

"Yep. Thought maybe that was what you were showing off to those other men, and that maybe you'd been wondering where it was."

"It was mine, yes. But that wasn't what I was showing to the other men."

"No?"

"No. I was showing them something else. You like pictures? Special pictures, if you know what I mean?"

"I don't think I do know what you mean."

The man reached a dirty hand into a pocket and produced a tintype that he put under Ben's nose. Ben arched his head back so he could see, and saw a lewd image of a naked woman. Some backstreet prostitute, most likely.

"Oh. That kind of picture."

"That's right." The man put the picture away. "But that tooth was mine. I didn't even realize I'd lost it. Guess it fell out of my pocket when I pulled out the picture."

"Where'd you get it?"

"Bought it off a man in St. Louis who has some women who work for him, if you know what I mean."

"I didn't mean the picture. The tooth."

"Why you care so much about a gold tooth?"

"Well . . . just interested."

"I found it. Lying on a road on the other side of town from here."

"Just one tooth?"

"Listen, friend, I don't know why you're asking me so many questions. I don't much like it. Why you so curious about a good tooth?"

A new voice spoke from behind Ben. "Bet I know." Ben turned and saw another of the group who had been examining the picture in the Cathedral. He had approached Ben unseen while he was talking to the first man. "There was a man murdered in Ferguson. His body was hauled in

102

this morning, and talk was he had gilded teeth. They'd all been pulled out.''

"Who are you?" Ben asked.

"Never mind who I am. I'm just me. And that man you're talking to there is my mining partner. And from what I'm hearing, seems to me you might be trying to find out if my good partner had something to do with that nigger's murder.''

"Look, all I'm trying to do is find out where that gold tooth came from. I don't know anything about any murder.''

"That's a lie. I saw you standing amongst the crowd around the corpse this morning. Seen you talking to the marshal.''

The first man, his manner emboldened now that he had a cohort, stepped closer to Ben, glaring. "You talked to a marshal? You tell him about the gold tooth you found?''

"Gentlemen, I regret I even brought the matter up. I'll be going on now.''

"No, you won't! Who are you, and why are you so interested in our affairs?''

"My name's Campbell. Harve Campbell. And I ain't interested at all anymore.''

"Your name ain't Campbell. Not if you're the brother of the man who owns that sleeping house. His name is Woolard.''

Ben said nothing, wondering what was going to happen.

"Give me back that tooth.''

"I can't. Don't have it on me.''

"Where is it, then?''

"I'll tell you," the second man said. "This morning he was claiming to the marshal that he'd give the tooth to a deputy earlier, for evidence.''

"I be damned! You're trying to get me tied in with some nigger murder! I don't much care for that, mister.''

"Look. My mistake. I'll forget about it. Good evening to you both.''

Ben turned and started to stride away. He wasn't surprised that it didn't work. One of the pair, he didn't see

103

who, jumped him from behind, and next thing he knew he was down, struggling, being beaten and kicked and generally abused, and though he fought back hard, it was two against one, and hopeless. As the sky darkened and evening descended, the struggle went on, silent but for the thuds and grunts and curses of the attackers.

It seemed to Ben that it continued for an inordinately long time.

Chapter Twelve

Jake's face in the lamplight was a fuzzy, vague imitation of itself, and no matter how many times Ben blinked his swollen eyes, it didn't seem to look quite right.

He could, however, easily make out Jake's forced smile, there, he figured, in an effort to make Ben feel that all was well, nothing really important had happened, that almost getting beaten to death at the edge of town didn't really amount to much.

"You know how to make an entrance, I'll grant you that," Jake was saying. "When Sally pulled open that door and we saw you standing there with blood and bruises and dirt all over you, we all just about fell over. I'm surprised you were able to stand at all."

"I don't even remember it," Ben said, as best he could with a swollen mouth.

"You seem to have an affinity for getting beaten up, brother of mine. This is twice since you've been in Ferguson, and this time Andy wasn't there to stop them before they knocked you senseless."

"Just lucky this time, I reckon."

"These men who did this to you, do you know their names?"

"No. Only their faces." He described them briefly.

"Why'd they do it?"

"Thought I was trying to accuse them of something. Jake, I don't much want to talk right now. Hurts."

"Fine. Keep quiet, and still. Rest up. We've got a doctor coming to look you over. And I'm going right now to talk to the marshal."

"No . . . no marshal."

"What happened to you was a crime, Ben. It ought to be reported."

"Not to this marshal."

"Why?"

"Don't like him . . . don't trust him, nor his deputies."

"Explain yourself, Ben."

"Later . . . when I can talk better."

Jake had a dark look. "I don't like this. You got something to hide from the law?"

"No. Trust me, Jake."

"I can at least fetch a doctor, can't I?"

"You can."

"Good. Because he's already on his way."

For a man who looked and felt as bad as he did, Ben was hurt surprisingly little. Nothing that would create any lasting damage, anyway. The doctor predicted several days of soreness and pain, followed by quickly diminishing discomfort and lessening stiffness. He asked pointed questions about how the injuries were inflicted, suggested that the law might need to be involved, then left. He'd say no more about it, get no further involved. In a town such as Ferguson, a man of medicine learned to mind his own business.

Ben slept after the doctor departed. When he awakened, Jake was at the bedside, dozing in a chair. Ben stirred a litle, seeking a better position, and felt a stab of full-body soreness that made him groan loudly. Jake awakened.

"Ben, you all right?"

106

"Hurting. Thirsty, too."

"I'll get you some water." He rose and disappeared, came back with cup in hand.

"So, you going to tell me about what happened?"

Ben relaxed and tried to quit hurting. He felt that maybe he could talk now, without too much difficulty. "You hear about the murder, the Negro fellow they found outside town?"

"I heard about it."

"It was Billy Platt. The brother of the teamster who gave me a ride into town. The one with the gold teeth."

"Yes. I know."

"I thought that one of these fellows maybe had something to do with it." He told, briefly, the story of the gold tooth and his visit with the fat deputy, and the attack that now had him laid up.

"Why didn't you leave it to the law?" Jake asked.

"Because it was clear that the law has no plan to do anything about it. That deputy denied I'd even brought him the tooth. And the marshal had no interest in anything I had to say."

"Still, it wasn't your affair."

"Jake, do you know who Roanie Platt believes killed his brother?"

"Who?"

"Henry Champion."

A pause, then a chuckle. "Champion? *The* Henry Champion?"

"The same."

"Why, for God's sake? It's absurd."

Ben took a deep breath and began to talk. He told the entire story, from Roanie's presence at the Champion hanging years ago, to Roanie's claim to have closely encountered Champion, alive and breathing, right here in Ferguson, to his own encounters with men who seemed to be Art Rellon and Jim Masker.

"So you believe this notion about Champion?" Jake asked.

Ben closed his eyes. "No. No. I know it isn't possible.

We saw the man die, you and me both. But Roanie seems convinced of it."

"And he saw Champion die, too."

"I know."

"The man doesn't have much sense, if he believes Champion is alive after having seen him hang with his own eyes."

"I know."

"Ben, you going to leave this thing alone now? Mind your own business?"

"I am."

"Good."

"Do you know, Jake, if the marshal still has Roanie in his custody?"

"No. I suppose we can find out come morning. It'll be in the newspaper, I guess."

"I guess." Ben felt very sleepy again. "Think I'll sleep some more. No need for you to sit up with me. Go on to your bed."

"Well, maybe I will."

"Jake . . . what about the Cathedral? Who's there tonight?"

"Your partner Hammel."

"Roscoe's doing it?"

"Yes. Andy went with him to explain the rules and so on. He didn't come back, so I expect Roscoe talked him into staying over, too."

"Never thought of Roscoe doing that job."

"Me either. But maybe I will now. If you're still wanting out, that is. He might make a good replacement for you whenever you do give it up for good."

Conversation dwindled, and Ben slept. He awakened late in the morning, very stiff and aching. He talked Sally into letting him look at himself in a handheld mirror, then groaned at what he saw.

"They might have killed you, Ben," she said.

"Looks to me like they did," threw in Judy, who was nibbling a biscuit and staring at him with undisguised fascination.

Ben was visited soon after by Roscoe and Andy, who scolded him playfully for taking such an extreme approach to getting out of mining labor.

"I'll be of little use to you for a couple of days, I'm afraid," Ben said.

"Longer than that, if you ask me. Hey, did we tell you? A woman came by the Cathedral last night, asking for you. Odd thing about it, she was dressed in a man's clothing. I don't think she meant for us to see that she wasn't a man. She came up and whispered to me while my back was turned, calling your name, and seemed mighty surprised when I turned around and she saw I wasn't you."

"Yeah. I know who you're talking about." Ben said no more, not wanting to advertise that he had violated the Cathedral rules more than once in allowing her to stay. "Did she say what she wanted?"

"No. Seemed mighty frightened. Like a scared rabbit, wasn't she, Roscoe? She turned and all but ran the other way."

Ben frowned, but it hurt and so he quit. "Did she seem scared before she realized that you weren't me, or just after?"

"Before, or so it seemed to me," Roscoe said. "I noticed her manner even before she spoke to Andy. Who is she, Ben?"

"Just a woman. A little bit crazy, maybe. I don't really know her, just talked to her a time or two."

Andy gave Ben a final gaze and shook his head. "My, my, but ain't you a sight! Well, Roscoe and me will be going. Doing our work and yours too."

"If you strike today, will you still share the wealth with me?"

"Oh, I reckon we'll give you a few dollars. You rest now. See you this evening."

Jake entered the room as Ben completed a delicious supper.

"Howdy, brother. Feeling all right?"

"Sore as can be. Stiff. Good food, though. You married yourself quite a cook."

"I know. Believe me." He patted his stomach. "Listen, Ben. I've done some asking around today, general questions and such. Talked to one of the deputies, not that same one you talked to. Couple of pieces of news for you."

Ben bit off a bite of bread. "I'm all ears."

"First off, the marshal let Roanie Platt go. He questioned him close, then decided there really was no good grounds for holding him, no reason to think he'd killed his own brother."

"I could have told them that."

"Yeah. Apparently a lot of people could, and did. Roanie Platt has an excellent reputation around this town. A good, levelheaded fellow. His brother, apparently, was the same sort."

Ben wondered how levelheaded Roanie really could be considering his conviction that a man long hanged and buried was at large and committing murder. "So where's Roanie now?"

"I don't know. Out trying to find the killer, probably. I doubt he expects the marshal to put forth much effort, and he's probably right. You know as well as I do that the death of a colored man doesn't count for much in the eyes of a lot of people."

"I know." Ben sipped his coffee.

"Now, another thing. It seems a pair of men matching the description you gave of the two who jumped you were seen leaving town this morning, early. Taking a wagon out and down the mountain."

"The deputy told you this?"

"No. I found it out all on my lonesome. Talking to an ore wagon driver, to tell the truth. Sort of an accident that I learned it. Anyway, this pair seemingly are a couple of no-accounts who'd drifted into Ferguson some days back, made a meager try at digging a few prospecting holes, but mostly just lay around the saloons and gambled. I'd say we'll not see them again. That means you won't be able to have them prosecuted, of course."

110

"That don't matter much. I'd rather have them gone, to tell the truth."

"Yeah. I'd feel the same. Anyhow, that's my news."

"I wonder what'll happen if Roanie finds whoever killed his brother."

"He won't find him. Can't. Not if he keeps with this notion that it was Henry Champion. Unless there's really such a thing as a ghost after all."

Ben passed a relatively comfortable night and the next morning became mobile again, however slowly and cautiously. He took advantage of Jake's wide porch, settling himself into a rocker, pillows stuffed around him here and there to make him more comfortable and to shield his many bruises. It was there that Roscoe Hammel found him when he stopped in at twilight, on his way from the mine to the Cathedral of Rest.

"Well, how's it feel to be following my old routine while I lay up like some lazy old sot, Roscoe?"

"Well, Ben, I don't much mind it. It lets me leave the mine a mite earlier, anyhow. Hey, we're missing you there. It ain't as easy with just two."

"Didn't seem much easy when there was three, to me."

"When you be back, you think?"

"Not long. I'm moving around pretty good. Not nearly as sore as I was. It was just a beating, after all. Nothing I ain't had before, and not as bad as it could have been."

"Hey, you had a visitor at the Cathedral last night."

"The woman?"

"If you mean the woman who wears the man's clothes and carries around that leather pouch, yes. She wouldn't tell me her name. She was coming hoping to find you."

"Her name's Deborah Bray. She's an odd woman. Very scared. Claims to have some sort of wicked brother who's trying to find her. That packet she has contains papers that will get him in some kind of trouble, she says, and he's supposedly searching around Ferguson to find her. That's why she disguises herself."

111

Roscoe had an odd look. "Now . . . what did you say that pouch had in it?"

"Papers of some sort. Legal documents, I suppose. Some kind of records or some such that will supposedly get this brother of hers in trouble with the law."

"I don't see how," Roscoe mumbled, as if to himself.

Ben frowned. "Roscoe, what do you know that you ain't saying?"

The big, gentle man suddenly looked guilty as Judas. He looked around, leaned over closer, and said, "Ben, you got to promise you won't tell your brother. I felt sorry for that woman, and I let her stay in the Cathedral last night."

"I'll bet you went and got her food, too."

"I did. She was nigh starved. How'd you know?"

"Because I've done the same thing for her myself. Don't tell Jake."

"I won't. But I'm glad to know it. She has a way of making you feel worried for her, don't she?"

"Indeed she does. But you talked like you knew something about those papers she carries."

Roscoe looked even guiltier. He dipped his head low. "Ben, I sneaked a look at them. I was just trying to find out her name, that's all. She wouldn't tell it to me, and I felt like I ought to at least know who she was, considering I was breaking the rules of the house for her. So I waited until she was sleeping, and I looked."

"Probably shouldn't have done that."

"I know."

"Well, what did you see?"

"Nothing. That's the strange thing. Them papers in that pouch, the ones you say are supposed to get this brother of hers in trouble, they was blank. Nothing written on them at all. Not a blessed word on a single one I looked at."

Chapter Thirteen

The next day, Ben took his first real walk since the beating. He was glad to know that his attackers were gone; he could roam Ferguson, as far as his sore body would let him, at least, without fear of turning a corner and coming face-to-face with them.

It was a beautiful day, the sky clear and blue, with that indescribable crystalline quality seen in the highest altitudes. Ben felt grateful to be alive, and even somewhat at home. An odd feeling, that one. He hadn't felt at home in years, no matter where he was, and he wasn't quite sure why he should feel at home now, in a town where he was still depending on his brother for security, and where he'd twice been pounded upon by strangers.

He was thinking of such things when he encountered her. Deborah Bray, still dressed in masculine fashion, was suddenly before him, and in his reverie he had failed to notice where she came from. The sudden appearance gave her a rather ghostlike quality, and he stared at her oddly.

"He's after me," she whispered. "Still chasing me, still planning to hurt me. I've seen him this very morning!"

"Your brother?"

"Yes! Yes! Who else?" She looked at Ben differently all at once, just then noticing his bruises and hobbling manner. "Merciful heaven! Has he gotten to you? Did my brother do this to you?"

"No. No. I just got into a row with some scoundrels. Deborah, listen to me. Are you sure that your brother is in town?"

"Of course!"

"And are you sure he's dangerous to you?"

"Why are you asking me this?"

Ben glanced down at the inevitable leather packet in her hands. "Is it those papers he's after?"

"Yes." She instinctively drew the packet close to her.

"Then why don't you find someone you can trust to turn the papers over to?"

"Because there *is* no one I can trust. I trust only you, Ben. And the nice man who has been at the Cathedral. He's kind, like you are. He let me stay, like you did."

"That's Roscoe. He is nice. He's also got a few doubts about your story. And I have to admit, so do I."

She looked betrayed, an expression so intense and pure it made Ben feel quite guilty. "Doubts? Why?"

Ben wasn't about to reveal that Roscoe had looked at her papers while she slept. He was beginning to develop a theory about this woman, and if it was accurate, he didn't want to give her reason to be angry at Roscoe. He wouldn't mention the blank papers.

"Because there's something odd in all this. Why do you keep roaming the same town, dressed the same way, supposedly running from the same man who nobody but you ever sees? . . . It just doesn't seem right."

"So you . . . you're one of them, too?"

"I'm not one of anybody. I'm just me, trying to figure out this wild story you keep telling, and the crazy way you behave. Listen to me, Deborah. If you need a place to stay, food and shelter, I believe I could help you. My brother is a prominent man here. He's also a kindhearted man, and he can probably find you a place to be, maybe even a way to support yourself until you get all ... all your problems worked out.''

''Would he hide me? From my brother?''

''I don't know ... maybe. He'd help you. I think ... you'll have to let me ask him. Tell him about you. Can I do that?''

She thought about it, holding the packet tight against herself. ''I'll tell you later.''

''When's later?''

''Tomorrow. I'll tell you tomorrow.''

''Where will I see you?''

''I'm going back to the Cathedral tonight. The nice man, Roscoe, he told me I could come back again. It's the only safe place for me. But I'm not sure it really is safe. I think maybe Daniel knows I've been staying there.''

Ben wondered if there really was a Daniel. He had strong doubts.

''I'm sure that Roscoe can keep you safe.''

''I hope so. He's such a kind, gentle man. So different from Daniel. There's nothing kind about my brother. Nothing gentle.''

She turned and was gone, vanishing into the crowd so fast that, again, she seemed ghostlike.

Ben shook his head, wondering if it was always this way in the thin atmosphere of a high mountain town. Was there something in the very air that brought out the bizarre in people and situations?

Turning slowly, he hobbled back toward Jake's house, fancying that he was moving a little more freely and easily than he had even an hour earlier. He hoped so; this being laid up and hobbling about like some old ancient got a man tired very quickly.

He was nearly to Jake's when he saw Marshal Fraley come stomping down the street, a shotgun in hand and a very upset Roanie Platt before him. The shotgun was poked right into the small of Roanie's back, and he was waving and gesturing and talking loudly and distraughtly, declaring that he ''knowed'' he'd ''made a mistake,'' that he was "sorry, and it ain't going to happen no more," he swore.

Ben frowned and wondered what was going on, then realized there was a third member of this little parade, a man trailing along behind the marshal. Ben turned his eyes to him.

He tensed so suddenly that every sore muscle in his body sent a throb of cramping pain through him.

The man was Henry Champion.

Henry Champion, sure as the world. Older, grayer, broader, but *him*!

Ben felt light-headed all at once. The world suddenly lost all its patterns and threw aside all its laws. Henry Champion was alive! It was impossible, yet there walked the evidence before him, on two thick legs. And if Champion could be alive, then the law of gravity could be suspended at any moment, two plus two might sometimes equal five, and a circle could be a square while still remaining a circle.

Then the object of Ben's astonished gaze turned his head and showed his face more clearly, and the world became sane again.

It wasn't Henry Champion at all. The resemblance was remarkable, but only at first glance. Now he saw that "Champion" was much bigger in the nose than the authentic item had been. And Henry Champion had never possessed ears that were out-thrusted and long-lobed. Further, Champion hadn't been nearly as barrel-chested as this fellow. Despite a healthy weight of muscle and bulk Champion had carried around on his frame, the frame itself had been entirely average in size. This man, however, had a rib cage that could accommodate a hogshead inside it.

Ben closed his eyes, took a deep breath, and trembled all over. Then he chuckled, and the day became brighter than ever.

All wondering was over now. Any subtle wondering about the possibility that maybe, somehow, Champion really was alive, now vanished.

It was all very clear. Roanie Platt had indeed seen a man he thought was Champion. The same fellow who now followed him and the marshal down the boardwalk. But it never had been Champion at all, just someone who resembled him.

Ben wondered what the story was behind the three-man parade that had just passed. Maybe Jake would know. As a merchant in an excellent position to hear every tale of the day, he seemed to know most everything that went on in the overgrown mining camp of Ferguson, Colorado.

Just as Ben hoped, Jake did know.

"Yes, I heard about that," he said over his well-laden plate at another late supper. "Really peculiar thing, but it makes sense of what you and I were talking about, Ben. It seems that Roanie Platt, once freed by the marshal after his first questioning, headed out determined to find Henry Champion for the murder of poor Billy Platt."

"Henry Champion!" Sally exclaimed. "But that's the name of the man who was hanged right after the war!"

"Yes, dear. I'll explain it all to you later. It's all a big misunderstanding on the part of one of our local Negroes, that's all. Anyway, Ben, Roanie went out, located this man who apparently does look a lot like an older version of Champion—"

"Yes, he does," Ben interrupted. "I saw him myself today, and almost fainted dead away. But when you take a closer look, you see he's quite a different fellow."

"Right. Apparently Roanie came to realize that, too, but only after he'd jumped the man and was about to beat him to death."

"Amazing. It's a good thing he realized his mistake in time."

"It is. It would have been a shame for a traveling preacher to have been beaten to death, mistaken for a long-dead bushwhacker."

"Preacher?"

"That's right. This fellow was a preacher. Just arrived in Ferguson ten minutes before Roanie Platt jumped him. Some kind of welcome, eh?"

"Yes." Ben grinned and returned to his supper. Old Roanie, getting everybody stirred up over nothing! Claiming that Henry Champion was around, when really it was nothing more than some old traveling Methodist, come to spread the gospel among the highland heathens.

"This old Christian, as I hear it, has decided to put his faith into his works and forgive poor old Roanie. He's not going to press an assault charge. But the marshal apparently is going to leave Roanie locked up overnight anyway, kind of a warning not to go jumping anybody else."

"Poor Roanie. He'll probably be laughed at from now on because of this."

"Yes. But sadder than that, this will probably make the marshal even less likely to really pursue whoever killed Billy Platt. The whole affair will seem like some sort of bother or foolishness to him, he'll forget the whole thing, and likely as not, Billy Platt's killer will never see any justice done to him."

"Is Roanie Platt that colored wagon driver?" young Judy asked.

"Yes, honey."

"Life isn't fair to colored people, is it?"

"No, honey. It's not."

Ben felt almost healed by the time he turned in that night. He was getting over the beating faster than he had hoped. As hard as the mine work was, he was almost eager to get back to it. Maybe he'd be able to tomorrow. . . . No, maybe not that soon. Maybe the next day.

Ben was almost asleep when he opened his eyes suddenly and frowned into the darkness. Earlier today, he'd mentally folded, boxed, and filed the case of Roanie Platt and Henry Champion, but new thoughts arose that suddenly threatened to make it come undone.

Like a cross-examining attorney, Ben's mind began asking him questions.

If Roanie's belief that Henry Champion was alive was to be explained by his having seen this preacher a time or two, and mistaking his identity, how was it that the preacher arrived only today, while Roanie has been claiming to have seen Champion well before that?

Also, what about Roanie's claim that Henry Champion

himself tried to assault him in the hills? The preacher wasn't in Ferguson then, and even if he was, would a preacher attack a man, or have cohorts do it?

It proved harder to get to sleep than Ben had anticipated.

Chapter Fourteen

The alarm sounded at three in the morning, a clanging, disruptive bell that pierced into the sleep of every resting denizen of Ferguson and told them that the most dreaded demon that could come to a mining town, just had.

Fire.

Ben sat up, blinking, trying to make sense of it. The bell clanged on. Jake, clad in a nightshirt, appeared at Ben's door, Andy just behind him, similarly dressed. Ben made out the shadowy figure of Sally, pulling a cloak around herself and the gown-clad, rounded form of young Judy.

Jake spoke. "There's a fire, Ben."

"Where?"

"I don't know."

Ben went to his bedroom window and looked out. "Jake . . . I can see the light of the fire. It's coming from the direction of the Cathedral."

"The Cathedral . . ."

Ben was hardly aware of his aches and pains as he dressed hurriedly and joined the general throng racing, like moths drawn to a giant candle, through dark streets and alleys toward the leaping, orange light that licked at the sky. Jake, Andy, and the rest of the family were already at the scene by the time Ben made it.

It was indeed the Cathedral. Flames shot through the high roof just as Ben arrived. The heat was intense, and the local fire brigade, working frantically, was concerning itself only with saving nearby buildings. The Cathedral itself was beyond hope.

One of Jake's fellow local merchants, clad, like most there, in trousers and nightshirt, came to Jake and touched his elbow. "I'm sorry, Jake. A big loss. And it's tragic, too, about that poor fellow."

"Oh, no . . . someone was still in there?"

"Only one, Jake. Only one. The rest got out. The only one trapped inside was the man you had overseeing it for you. So I'm told by those who've gotten out."

"Roscoe . . ." Ben whispered. He stared, disbelieving, at the hellish flame and felt sick. "Roscoe. No!" Part of him said to lunge forward, find Roscoe, and somehow pull him out of the burning building. Another part told him how foolish and hopeless that would be. He couldn't even draw close to such an inferno, much less enter it. And Roscoe by now would be beyond all help. Gone.

So Ben did nothing but stand like a statue, staring at the flames until they seared their light into his eyes and were still visible even when he closed his eyes and at last turned away.

She was there, beside him. Again she had appeared in phantomlike fashion. She was in the same clothes as always, but much more dirty, covered with ash and soot and smelling of smoke.

"You're alive," Ben said softly. "You were inside?"

"Yes. It was Daniel. Daniel set this blaze."

"How do you know?"

"Because I saw him."

Ben frowned. "You saw him? He was inside the place?"

"No. Outside. He set the fire in the alley, against the building. I saw him there."

"Deborah, I'm trying not to doubt you"—though he did

indeed doubt her strongly—"but I'm not understanding something. There was no window in the overseer's sleeping chamber. So how could you see into the alley from inside?"

"Through the knotholes. There were two knotholes through the wall, on the side looking out onto the alley. I heard a noise in the alley, smelled smoke, and looked out and saw him through the knotholes."

Ben tried to remember whether there had in fact been knotholes in that wall. He couldn't, try as he would. But if there had been knotholes, it would have been possible to look out through them directly into the alley. The pine walls of the Cathedral of Rest had been only one board thick.

Another soot-covered figure, apparently a survivor of the blaze, approached Ben and Deborah. He put out his hand to her. "I wanted to thank you, sir, for giving the alarm. If you hadn't, we'd all have died."

This man obviously took Deborah's male garb at face value, believing her a male. He was far too distracted at the moment to look closely enough to see his error. Deborah smiled at him, made a guttural grunting noise of affirmation, and quickly shook his hand.

If he noticed that the hand was unusually slender, it didn't show in his reaction. "I owe you my life, mister," he said, and turned away.

Ben said, "You fooled him, at least. So it was you who gave the first alarm?"

"Yes. I yelled. With my voice as low as I could make it sound. Roscoe was the first to wake up. He stirred the others and got them out. All out . . . all but Roscoe himself."

Ben lowered his head and felt tears rise. Embarrassed to cry before her, he quickly brought himself under control, dabbed his cheek very fast, and looked up at her again. She was not crying. He could not read her face at all.

"I suppose it gives credence to what you said, that man saying you were the first to give the alarm."

"Did you doubt what I said?"

"I don't remember seeing any knotholes in that wall, that's all."

"Did you ever look?"

"No."

"Then you don't know that there weren't any. And I'm telling you that there were." She sounded perturbed. He didn't blame her.

The fire brigade began pushing the crowd back. Ben grasped her elbow and moved her along with him, not wanting to lose her before he had a chance for some further conversation. It was time for some answers. He moved all the way across the street and into the shadows, getting out of the light of the fire and away from the likely earshot of anyone else.

"I want you to answer a question for me. That packet you carry, the papers you said would implicate your brother in the murder of your father—why were those papers blank?"

"Blank?" She frowned. "What do you mean?"

"The papers. There was nothing written on them."

"You *looked* at my papers? My private papers?"

"No. But Roscoe did. Maybe he shouldn't have, but he did. And he told me there was nothing written on them."

"He was wrong. There were letters in that packet. Documents."

"Why would Roscoe lie to me?"

"He didn't."

"Mercy, woman—talking to you is like talking to a walking riddle! Either those papers were blank, and you've been lying about them, or they had something written on them. Which was it?"

"Both. The documents were hidden in the lining. Most of the rest of the paper was blank. Stationery."

Ben thought about it. Again, it made sense . . . maybe. Like the knothole story, he couldn't say it was true, but neither could he say it was false. Roscoe had looked through the packet in pressured circumstances. And the man, noble as he had been, hadn't been the smartest of fellows. Maybe he'd just not looked closely or deeply enough to find the written material.

"Where is the packet now?" Ben asked.

She glanced toward the burning warehouse, now thoroughly engulfed in flames. Most of the roof fell in even as she watched, sparks and flame shooting to an incredible height as it happened and making every onlooker cringe and pull away.

"Deborah, I'm going to ask you something, and I want an honest answer from you. Is the story you've told me, about your murdered father, and your half brother, and the documents and the danger you're in—is that story true?"

She looked him squarely in the eye. "It is true."

"Every word?"

"Every word."

"Swear to God above?"

She lifted her hand. "I swear before God." She lowered her hand. "Do you believe me?"

He took in a deep breath and let it out slowly. Finally he nodded. "I believe you."

One of the walls of the Cathedral fell in, sending out another explosion of flame, sparks, and heat, causing the crowd to gasp as one and pull back even farther. The heat was baking, the light dazzling. Ben squinted into the brilliance, entranced by it, horrified as well, thinking how dreadful it must have been for poor Roscoe to die in such a place. The tears rose again, drying on his face even as they fell, evaporated away by the intense, attacking heat.

He watched the fire a while longer, then turned to speak to Deborah.

She was gone.

They buried Roscoe Hammel, or what bits of charred bone remained of him, in the graveyard outside of town. Far more people stood at his graveside than would have been there had he died like most who filled this cemetery, of accident or illness. Roscoe Hammel had died a grander death, a heroic death, died while making sure the men under his charge safely escaped. And so the people came to see him laid away.

But when the grave was filled, they dispersed, and Ben stood beside Andy, Jake, and the other Woolards, and knew that before long Roscoe would be forgotten. The blackened rubble of the Cathedral would be cleared away, and Jake would put up some other business, or sell the lot to somebody else who would. Before long the fire would be forgotten and the man who died in it would become a distant memory.

It seemed to Ben a sort of analogy of life itself. Men were born, live, thought themselves and their tasks important, but suddenly it ended, one way or another, and the men and their lives were forgotten. No longer mattered. The world progressed without them, filled with new people operating under the same delusions of significance as the others before them, now forgotten, now moldering away in their graves.

Or so it all seemed to Ben Woolard just now, and so it was that when evening came, he was seated not at Jake and Sally's supper table, as usual, but in one of the local saloons, staring at a brown bottle of cheap whiskey purchased an hour before. Purchased but so far not imbibed from.

Ben longed to open that bottle and take a drink. Then another, and another, and forget about the fire, about life and loss and suffering. The death of Roscoe had done something to him, opened wounds left by the death of his own family, wounds that had only recently begun to heal over enough to let him get on with living.

Now he wasn't sure living was worth it. Maybe he'd been right to turn to liquor after he lost his wife and children. Maybe it made more sense to numb one's self to life rather than subject one's self, unprotected, to its tortures.

He reached for the bottle.

"Ben, I hope you don't do what I think you might be about to do."

Ben looked up at the man who had approached him from the side. He smiled without mirth and chuckled without pleasure. "Sit down, Andy. Care to join me for a drink?"

126

Andy looked at the bottle. "Maybe I will at that." He scooted out the chair opposite Ben and settled into it. He looked closely at the bottle, then at Ben, beyond it.

"You and me have both about drowned in that stuff, Ben."

"Yep."

"Right now drowning don't seem such a bad thing."

"Nope."

"How long you been sitting here?"

"I don't know. An hour."

"So why ain't you took a drink?"

"I don't know as I can answer that."

"Maybe because down deep you don't really want to."

"Maybe. What about you? You want to?"

"I do. And I don't. Because, you know, even if I take it, and get good and drunk so that it doesn't hurt to think about Roscoe, when I come out of it on the other side, the hurting's going to still be there, and Roscoe's going to still be gone."

"Good point."

"So if we ain't going to drink, what are we going to do?"

"What do you mean?"

"What are we going to do? For Roscoe?"

Ben crossed his arms before him on the table and lowered his chin onto them in the fashion of a bored schoolboy, and stared into the amber bottle, looking at the distorted image of Andy on the other side of it.

"Well, the only thing I could think of to do for Roscoe would be to find the person who set that blaze, and see him punished for what he did."

"I been thinking along the same lines. But we don't know how it started. Might have caught on fire by accident."

"Seemed to me I smelled a bit of coal oil in the air during that blaze."

"So did I."

"Besides, I talked to a woman who said she saw a man setting it. She was inside the place, and said she looked out through knotholes in the wall of the overseer's sleeping chamber, and saw the man doing it."

"A woman? In the overseer's chamber? Wait a minute . . . you're saying Roscoe had a woman with him? *Roscoe?*"

"No. He was sleeping out in the main section, and let her stay in his bed. Alone. He did it because he felt sorry for her. It was against house rules, of course, but he did it, and the truth is, I'd done the very same myself a time or two before. Same woman. I'd just as soon you not tell your father. Not that it really matters now. By the way, do you remember there being any knotholes in the wall at the overseer's chamber?"

"There were two or three, as I recall."

"So she was telling the truth about that. I guess she was probably telling the truth about the rest, too."

"What was the rest?"

"That the man who set the blaze did it because he knew she was somewhere inside, and wanted to kill her. Her name's Bray. Deborah Bray. The man who set the fire, according to her, is named Daniel Bray. Her half brother."

"You telling me straight? Her half brother?"

"That's right. And he's supposedly killed before. Their own father."

"Sounds like quite a fearsome devil, this Daniel Bray."

"He murdered Roscoe. That's what matters most to me. And he may murder Deborah, if he finds her. I wish I could find her first. Take her somewhere safe and protect her. But she has a way of appearing and disappearing, and right now I have no notion about where she might be."

Andy frowned into the amber, thoughtful. "Ben, I got an idea. Why don't we leave this whiskey sitting right where it is, and get out of here. And then why don't we lay aside mining for a while, and spend a bit of time looking for this Daniel Bray. See if we can't catch him and make him pay—by the law or outside it, I don't care which—for killing poor old Roscoe? What do you say?"

"I say it sounds good to me."

"You up to it? Healed up enough from that beating?"

"I'm up to it. And I'm going to do it even if I ain't up to it."

"Let's go find that son of a bitch."

"Let's do. And let's find Deborah, too. It's important to me to find her."

"Pretty woman?"

"Very much so, as best as I can tell. I ain't seen her a time except that she's been dressed in a man's clothes."

"What? Why?"

"To disguise herself from her brother."

"Sounds like sort of a strange kind of woman."

"She is. I've wondered a time or two if she's sane. But as it appears right now, she's been telling me the truth all along. I believe she's who she says, and what she says, and I believe she's in true danger from her own brother."

"Let's go do something about it."

"Let's do."

"Should we go have a word with the marshal?"

"I don't like the marshal. I don't trust the marshal."

"Neither do I."

They stood and walked out. In a crowded mining town saloon, a full bottle left unguarded at an empty table wouldn't remain where it was long, and theirs did not. It was picked up almost immediately by a broadly built, gray-haired man who had been watching that table, unnoticed, from the shadowed corner since long before Andy joined Ben. The bottle in his hand, he sauntered slowly to the door of the saloon and looked out into the falling evening, watching the pair walk off together, and merge into the ever-present milling crowds of Ferguson.

Chapter Fifteen

Jake Woolard loosened his collar, tugged and adjusted his armbands, and slipped off to the back room of his store, gently closing the door behind him, and even more gently settling a locking bar into place.

Once alone, he grimaced, yawned, stretched, and listened to his joints pop. Lord, what a day! Busy from the moment he opened. His back ached from having unloaded a new shipment of mining supplies earlier in the morning, and with a lunch freshly settled in his stomach and store traffic momentarily diminished, he was ready to do something he did more often than he would want anyone to know: Leave the store momentarily in the hands of his two clerks outside, and stretch out for a few moments of rest on a cot nicely hidden behind stacked crates here in the storeroom.

The clerks knew what he did, and he knew that they knew, but the accepted approach was for them to pretend they didn't, while he pretended, in turn, that he didn't know they were pretending. Easier all around that way. He suspected that the clerks were just as glad to have the boss out of their hair for half an hour each afternoon as he was to escape the labor of merchantry for those same blissful minutes.

He stretched out on the bunk and wondered if this daily need for a nap had anything to do with getting older. No. Surely not.

Jake drifted soon into a pleasant but odd dream, something involving drifting along on a cloud high above the mountains, enjoying the risky feeling of flight while also knowing that, no matter what, he couldn't really fall, when a bumping sound on the other side of the wall jolted him awake.

He opened his eyes and glared at the ceiling. Somebody was out in the alley, just behind the storeroom. Oh, well. Folks in Ferguson walked everywhere, through yards and alleys as much as down the street and boardwalks. He closed his eyes again. Another bump.

This time he sat up, realizing that the bump came from an area of the alley that he had enclosed with a wooden fence built up against his building, a place he could set out trash and so on without fear that dogs or wildlife would get into it. Something, apparently, had gotten inside the fence.

Blasted clerks! How many times had he told them to make sure they closed the gate securely after putting out refuse?

A small, high window looked out into the fenced area. He got up from the bunk and stepped onto a crate, bringing his face up to the window. He looked out in anticipation of seeing a dog knocking about in the garbage.

He had barely gotten his face up to the glass when another face appeared on the other side of it. A man's face, inches from his own, separated from his only by the thin glass.

Jake yelled and fell back off the crate, landing on his rump on the storeroom floor. He looked up wildly at the window. The man was gone.

Both clerks rattled the barred storeroom door. ''Mr. Woolard? What was that noise? Are you all right?''

The door burst open on them and Jake Woolard came

out on a run, heading through the store, around the front, into the alley. . . .

The gate on the high fence was open, creaking and swinging in the wind. The man who had been in there was gone, having fled very quickly, maybe as startled to have seen Jake's face as Jake had been startled to see his.

Jake stopped and gazed at the open gate. He panted like a dog. Having gone so quickly from rest to violent motion, with a good scare thrown in besides, had left him winded.

The clerks pounded around the corner and up to him. "Mr. Woolard? What in the world is going on?"

Jake continued to stare at the open gate. He said nothing.

"Mr. Woolard?"

"You fellows need to be careful to keep that gate closed," he said. "I've told you time and again."

He turned and walked back up the alley, leaving them frowning and puzzled. They looked at each other; one of them shrugged. The other walked to the gate and closed it, checking it to make sure it was securely closed.

"I suppose the boss man's nap is through for today," he said as he rejoined the other.

"I suppose so. I wonder what that was all about."

"We'll likely never know."

Jake was unusually silent at supper that night, but none of the others particularly noticed. All were in a pensive mood, except perhaps for Judy, who as the youngest was the least understanding and least affected by the terrible death of Roscoe Hammel, to her a virtual stranger despite his frequent visits to this very table.

With the Cathedral gone there were no Woolard beds to be had except those in the house itself. Ben volunteered to make a pallet on the floor for himself, but Andy quickly overrode that idea, pointing out that Ben was still bruised up from his beating. And besides, he noted, he'd gotten awfully used to sleeping on floors during his drinking days.

Ben and Andy said nothing to Jake about their plans to seek out Daniel Bray. They were unsure what he would think about their putting aside their mining in a project that he had grubstaked with his own dollars and equipment. They were even more unsure how he would take to the idea of their effectively taking the law in their hands and searching for a criminal on their own, rather than through the official channels.

Their silence, though, was unnecessary. Jake was in no mental state to even think about the mine or his grubstake, or even who had set fire to the Cathedral. He had another thing to occupy him, something he wasn't sure he would share even with his own wife. It seemed too absurd.

But that night he did share it. Rolling over and facing her in the darkness, he stirred her from the edge of sleep with a question. "Sally, why do you think a man would sneak into an alley and peak into the back window of a general mercantile's storeroom?"

She lifted her head slightly from her pillow. "That happened?"

"Yes. Today. I heard something bumping around in the alley, back where the fence is, and looked out that little window to see what it was. I figured I'd see a dog, but it wasn't. It was a man, and he stuck his face up to the window at the same time I did. Almost scared me to death!"

Her face was invisible to him in the darkness, but he could tell that he had just worried her. "That's strange, Jake," she said.

"I know. And it's been on my mind ever since. Why do you think somebody would do a thing like that?"

She paused, then said, "I'd as soon not think it, but the first thing that comes to mind is that they might be thinking of robbing the place. Maybe he was looking for a way to get inside after dark."

"I've thought just the same. But I've also wondered if maybe he was looking inside not so much to see into the store itself, but to see if he could see *somebody* who was in the store."

"Well, I suppose. But it seems an unlikely explanation, to tell you the truth. Robbery seems a more likely one." She hesitated. "Oh, Jake . . . what if somebody's down there now, robbing the place?"

"I had a word with the marshal today about it. Asked him to have a deputy keep an eye on the store after dark for two or three days. He said he'd do that."

"Good." She settled back down again, but sleep wouldn't come for a while now. She had unsettling things to mull. After a few moments, she asked, "Jake, why did you say that about somebody trying to see a person inside the store? I mean, what made something like that come to mind?"

There was an answer to that question, but he didn't want to tell it to her. It seemed too foolish and impossible, too close to notions he'd already derided to his own brother not long before. "Oh, it was just a silly thought, that's all. You know how things like that can get your mind to thinking crazy things." He leaned across and kissed her. "Good night, sweetheart."

"Good night. I love you."

Ben, having declared himself fit to work, left with Andy the next morning as if they were going together to the mine. They diverted course once out of sight of the house, and realized they weren't quite sure how to proceed from there.

"We won't keep this hidden from Pa for long, you know," Andy said. "The town is his domain, and we'll not spend much time poking around for this Bray fellow without it getting back to him."

"I know," Ben replied. "That's why I hope it doesn't take us long to find him. But it isn't just Daniel Bray we'll be looking for. We've got to find Deborah Bray, too."

"Where do you think she's gone?"

"I don't know. She tends to appear and disappear at will."

"Or against her will."

Ben thought about it. "Andy, you thinking that maybe he's got her?"

"You'll never know without looking. So let's look."

And as the day rolled past, look they did. Ben had no idea where Deborah spent her time. Did she roam the streets? Settle into the background in the saloons and cafes? Hide in the alleys and rows?

The question was no nearer an answer when, in late afternoon, a weary Ben Woolard began to suspect he'd not find Deborah Bray that day at all. He'd spent exhausting, dull hours roaming and looking, staring at strangers, trying to examine the inhabitants of the shadowy rears of cafés and drinking houses. So far he'd seen no sight of Deborah.

But as he began to wind his way back toward Jake's house, his still-healing body now very sore from the day's exertion, he did see Roanie Platt, crossing the street ahead of him.

"Roanie!" he called. "Roanie! Hold up!"

The black man turned a solemn face toward him, eyes narrowing. No smile, no glimmer of gold. For a moment Ben thought that Roanie was angry, but as he drew closer he saw that his expression was more one of sorrow. And frustration.

"Roanie, good to see you free."

"Thank you, sir. No reason I shouldn't be free. I ain't done a wrong thing. None but one, anyhow."

"The one being that you attacked a preacher that you thought was Henry Champion. Right?"

"That's right, sir. He looked a right smart like him, so much you'd think it was the same man just to glance at him."

"I know. I happened to see the same fellow while he was following you and the marshal down the street."

"Yeah. Humiliating, that was, sir. But I believe the marshal likes to humiliate me. I don't find he thinks very high of a colored man."

"Roanie, I need to know something. Your talk about Henry Champion . . . was all of that just a mistake, like the mistake about the preacher? Maybe somebody who just looked like Champion?"

Roanie shook his head firmly. "No, sir. No, sir. Not at all. The business with the preacher was a mistake, and I admit it. But Henry Champion is here, sir. He *is*. Impossible as it seems. I swear it."

Ben had hoped that Roanie wouldn't say that.

"And it ain't only Champion who's alive, sir. There's some of his old gang with him. After all these years, still with him!"

"Who?"

"One name of Rellon, sir. Arthur Rellon. And another called Masker. I don't know his first name."

"Jim," Ben said, his heart sinking inside him. "His name is Jim Masker. And I think I've seen him."

Roanie actually brightened. "Then you believe me, sir, about Henry Champion?"

"Roanie . . . I don't know what to believe. It's one thing to see Jim Masker or Arthur Rellon alive. Nobody ever hanged them, after all. But Champion is a different matter. We both saw him die. You and me. And my brother saw it, too. He can't be alive."

"Can't be . . . but he is. And he murdered Billy, and pulled out all his teeth."

"Do you have any evidence besides your own claims?"

"Yes, sir," Roanie replied. "It so happens that I do. There's an old fellow out in the mountains, a prospector who's struck a bit of silver here and there, and lives now up under Goatbeard." The reference was to a certain peak in the vicinity with an undercrop that many fancied bore a resemblance to the beard of a goat. "This man, I'm told, knows for a fact that Champion and some of his old gang are here. And he knows where he's staying."

"You talked to this man yourself?"

"No."

"You aim to?"

"I do. You want to come with me, sir?"

Ben found himself actually considering it, but after a few moments of thought he shook his head. "No, Roanie. I don't believe I will. To tell you the truth, the notion of Champion being alive is one I ain't too keen to explore too much. It bothers me just to think of it. Besides, it ain't possible. Whatever you think we saw in that prison yard, I *know* what I saw. I saw a man hanged until he was dead."

Roanie looked at him in a way that, oddly, made him

feel he had just said the most hurtful and irresponsible words possible. So he went further, explaining. "But the real reason, Roanie, is that I've got something else that has to be done now, something more pressing to me than searching for bushwhacker ghosts. I'm trying to find somebody who may be in bad trouble. Maybe in danger of her life."

"A woman, huh?"

"That's right."

"Your woman, sir?"

"No. Not really. Just a . . . friend."

Roanie nodded. "Friends is important, sir. I hope you find her."

Roanie turned and walked away, shoulders slumped.

Chapter Sixteen

"Wonder where Andy is," Jake said for the third time since the meal had begun.

Ben glanced at Sally and saw the worried puzzlement in her eyes as she watched her husband. Indeed Jake wasn't himself. He was distracted and seemed quite worried. About Andy? Probably, but Ben figured there was more to it than that. Andy had been late for supper many a time, had missed suppers entirely during his time of drinking, with Jake not getting nearly as distracted as he was now.

"I expect Andy'll show up anytime now," Ben said, the same answer he'd given the first two times Jake had asked.

"I hope he ain't drunk again," Judy said, filling her mouth with potatoes.

"Judy, don't talk that way. Andy has given up his drinking."

"Sometimes people go back to drinking, though. Ain't that right, Uncle Ben?"

Ben said, "Well, I guess so."

"Like you. I bet you'd like to go back to drinking sometimes when you think about your dead family, wouldn't you?"

139

"Judy!" Sally erupted. "Good lands, child, have you no notion of other people's feelings?"

Judy looked more unhappy at being scolded than sorrowful. She delved back into her food and shut out the world around her.

Sally grimaced at Ben. "I'm sorry."

"Never mind. The fact is, Judy's right. A man does think about drinking sometimes, once he's got himself used to it. The fact is, I was sore tempted because of what happened to poor Roscoe. But I didn't touch a drop, and I'm glad of it."

Jake, who normally would have been deeply involved in such a conversation, sat silent, lost in his own thoughts, his brows knitted.

They ate a while longer. Jake said, "I wonder where Andy is."

Sally and Ben glanced at each other again. Judy kept eating.

Sally found Jake alone in the backyard after supper. He paced and smoked, staring at the sky, the mountains, the ugly lumber-colored backsides of the nearest buildings.

"Jake, you've got to talk to me. Something's wrong."

He looked at her as if she were a stranger, still frowning.

"For heaven's sake, Jake! What is it?"

"It's Andy. I'm worried about why he isn't home yet."

"It is not Andy. He's a grown man, and you never worried this much even when he was at his worst. There's more to it than that, and I want you to tell me."

He considered it, drawing slowly on his cigar, then tossing it to the ground. He stared at the red coal as it flickered and sizzled in the evening damp. "Nothing. Really, honey, it's nothing. I'm just tired. Maybe coming down with a spell of sickness."

"I don't believe it. I think this has to do with that man who looked into the storeroom window. Am I right?"

"No. It's just that I'm feeling sort of sickly. Nothing bad. That's all."

She looked at him closely. "Are you sure, dear?"

He smiled. "Of course. Don't worry. I'm sorry I've acted this way. And I do wish Andy would come home."

Her manner warmed and she came to him, wrapping her arm around him. "Andy'll be in later. And if you're feeling sick, you ought to get inside and go to bed early. Get some extra sleep. I'll tell you when Andy gets home."

"All right." He hugged her. "I love you, dear. I wouldn't know what to do if I lost you."

"Then don't lose me."

Ben's confidence that Andy would soon return faded as the evening dragged on. Tired as he was, he didn't go to bed when he wanted, but instead went to the porch and planted himself there, looking out into town and waiting to see Andy appear.

Jake joined him about ten o'clock. "Thought you were in bed, Ben."

"No. Kind of wanting to see Andy get home, you know."

"Me, too." Jake sat down in a rocker and stared over the porch rail. "Ben, let me make mention of something. Did I tell you about what happened at the store yesterday— me catching a fellow looking in through the storeroom window off the alley?"

"No."

Jake related the story succinctly. Ben voiced the obvious concern that the man might have been looking the place over in anticipation of a robbery.

"I don't think that's it, Ben. I truly don't. There's something about that man that I haven't mentioned to Sally. Or to anyone else, either." He hesitated. "I knew the fellow. It was Bill Helm."

Ben sucked in his breath, a little more loudly than he wished. "Bill Helm . . . *the* Bill Helm?"

"The one who rode with Henry Champion, yes. The one who sat through every minute of that trial, and had to be carried off by soldiers to keep him from barging in on the hanging, yes."

Ben felt cold all at once. "That makes three, Jake. Three

141

men who either happen to look just like some of Champion's gang, or three who really *were* some of Champion's gang. And all here in the same town, the same one where a colored teamster swears that Henry Champion himself is alive, too.''

"You're talking about Roanie Platt?"

"Yes. I spoke to him again this very day. Jake, he swears that Champion is alive and here. He says the preacher he mistook for Champion isn't the same man he's seen before. It was coincidence, he says, just a mistake. And that has to be true. I got to thinking about this here lately. Roanie's been claiming to have seen Champion since well before the preacher he mistook for him even got to town.''

"But what can it mean, Ben? And how can it be? Even if some of Champion's old bushwhackers are here, that can't explain how a dead man can be walking again.''

"I know. Which is what I always come back around to. No matter how odd it seems, it can't be Champion, because Champion is dead and buried.''

Conversation lagged. Both men rocked fast, tensely, staring into the darkness and looking for Andy.

"Ben, why would Bill Helm be looking into my storeroom window?''

"Maybe thinking to rob it, like I said.''

"Or maybe he was looking in hopes of seeing me. Seeing if the Woolard who runs the mercantile in Ferguson is either of the Woolards who helped put Henry Champion on the gallows.''

"Maybe.''

"Which means there could be danger. It might be more than mere curiosity. Helm might have notions of avenging his old partner. He was devoted to Champion, you know.''

"Yes." Ben played through his mind an almost-forgotten image—Bill Helm being dragged away from the Nashville prison yard, his arms and legs flailing, screaming curses and all but weeping as he demanded to be allowed to witness the execution of the murderous bushwhacker whom he had called friend. Ben had never known what became of Bill Helm after that.

Maybe now he did.

Ben rocked and thought. The night seemed more ominous than before. At length he said, "Blast it, Jake, I'm not going to let myself get eaten up over all this. Champion's dead. So is the past, and I'm not going to spend my time looking over my shoulder for it to jump up like some spook or booger and yell 'Boo!' I'll not do it!"

Jake listened to the impassioned talk, flipped his brows up to show he was impressed, then smiled slightly. "All right, then. I reckon that's settled. So, how's mining?"

"Well, to tell you the truth, Andy and I didn't do any mining today."

"Why not?"

"We spent the day looking for somebody. A woman I met."

"A woman!"

"Why do you sound so surprised? I might begin to feel insulted."

"I just . . . I don't know. I didn't think you were to the point of looking at other women yet. After what you went through."

"The truth is, I'm not looking, not in *that* way. This isn't what it sounded like. The reason I'm looking for her is that she might be in danger. She claims to be, anyway."

"What kind of danger?"

"She's hiding from a brother she claims killed their father. A half brother, actually. She says she's seen him in Ferguson, and all at once I can't find her."

"How'd you meet up with her in the first place?"

"Just a chance meeting, that's all." He saw nothing to be gained in telling the full tale of how she slept unauthorized in the Cathedral.

"When you find her, what are you going to do?"

Ben realized he didn't have an answer. He'd thought no farther than simply finding her and making sure she was all right. "I don't know," he admitted.

"Well, if I can help her in any way, let me know," Jake said.

Ben smiled his appreciation and wondered if Jake would be so magnanimous if he knew that it might have been to kill her that his Cathedral of Rest was torched.

"What's her name?" Jake asked.

"Deborah Bray."

"What's she look like?"

"A man."

"Huh?"

Ben chuckled. "She looks like a man because she's been dressing as one to throw her brother off her trail. His name is Daniel Bray, incidentally. If you should happen to run across him or hear of him somewhere, let me know."

"You really believe he's a danger to her?"

Ben paused, then nodded. "There's been times I've wondered about her, how stable and truthful she is . . . but yes. I do believe her. My gut says she's truly in danger. Andy is helping me look for her, by the way."

Jake nodded. "That makes me wonder all the more where he might be. You think this Daniel Bray might have done something to him?"

"The thought has crossed my mind, and it ain't a welcome one. I'd feel awful, pit-of-hell awful, if anything bad happened to that young man because of me."

And just then, as fate would have it, they saw him. Andy trotted into the yard and up to the porch. Breathless, he nodded a quick greeting to his father and said to Ben, "I need a private word."

"Have you found her?"

Andy looked surprised and cut his eyes quickly toward his father.

"It's all right," Ben said. "I told him about her. Did you find her?"

"No, but I found a man who claims he knows where she is. Or, at least, someone who fits her description. He's in town right now, half drunk, and waiting for us. We need to talk to him tonight, Ben, or else we may lose our chance. He seems a shiftless kind."

144

Jake asked, "Is she in danger, Andy?"

Andy, no doubt wondering if Ben had told his father *everything,* including Deborah Bray's possible connection to the Cathedral fire, said, "She might be."

"How?"

"This man, he's told me little so far, demanding that I give him more money—and I've already cleaned out my pockets for him. But he's hinted around some, and I believe what he's going to tell us is that Daniel Bray has found her, and maybe taken her away."

Ben whispered a curse and came to his feet.

"Ben . . . take this," Jake said, handing him something. Ben took it. A small pistol, compact enough to lie fully on a big man's hand. "I wanted to give it to you anyway . . . just in case the other business we talked about has something to it."

Ben took the pistol. "Thank you. I will take it. But not because of Champion. That's a figment, nothing more. The man I'm concerned about is flesh and blood, and I hope to God we're not too late. I hope to God he hasn't done anything to Deborah."

Chapter Seventeen

A "figment," Ben had called Champion. Now it seemed that the knowledgeable man Andy had claimed to find was a figment as well.

"He was here, I swear," Andy said, looking around the crowded saloon, thick with out-of-tune piano music and blue-tinted, reeking clouds of smoke. "He said he'd stay right there, in that chair, until I got back."

"Well, he didn't, obviously. How much money did you give him?"

"All I had on me. Ten dollars."

"He's gone off to some other saloon, I'll bet you. Off buying himself more liquor."

They began a saloon-to-saloon search that ate up more than an hour, but the man could not be found. Discouraged, they headed back to Jake's house, weary and swearing to try again the next morning. Jake was still up, still on the porch.

"Any luck?"

"He was gone."

Jake didn't seem surprised.

Ben slept very little that night. It seemed absurd to be lying in bed, trying to rest, when there was no telling what Daniel Bray might be doing to Deborah. Even now he might be lifting a pistol to her forehead in some lonely mountain spot. Or maybe throwing a noose over a limb, or laying out a wrist for slitting. Maybe the act was already done, and he was disposing of the body.

Finally Ben did sleep, somehow, and awakened early the next morning ready to begin again. Andy, who had slept well, was rested and vigorous, and apologetic for having let his informant disappear.

"It was a foolish mistake, and I won't make another one like it again."

"What was this fellow's name?"

"He wouldn't say. But I'll know his face."

Four hours later, the town of Ferguson had been pretty thoroughly scoured, and that face hadn't shown itself. "I'm thinking we may have hit a wall," Ben said. "This man probably has moved on. And I'm betting he didn't really know anything. He just strung you along for the money."

Andy said nothing, and Ben figured he'd just inadvertently insulted his nephew. But he hoped he was right, and that the man really didn't know of any harm coming to Deborah. He'd rather know nothing of her whereabouts than to know that anything bad had come her way.

They found the man as soon as they stopped looking for him.

Ben was the first to spot him, and though he hadn't laid eyes on the man before, something about him caused him to look twice, and point him out to Andy.

"That's him!" Andy declared. "You! Hey, there! Stop right there!"

Andy raced forward with such fervor that Ben expected the man to pee his pants and take off on a run. But instead the fellow stayed where he was, looking dumbly at Andy from beneath heavy gray brows. Ben followed Andy along the boardwalk, hobbling a little and not quite as fast.

By the time Ben got there, Andy was already quizzing

the man intensely, and scolding him at the same time for his failure to be where he said he would be the night before. The man, a small and frail-looking fellow, age hard to determine because of the effects of drinking, seemed to be having trouble remembering a thing about the prior night.

But as Ben stood by and listened to Andy pummel the fellow with questions, comprehension began to dawn in the thin face. At last the man put on a look of great concern, and said, "Many pardons, friends, many pardons.... The fact is I wasn't feeling well last night, took a bit of medicine to help me sleep, and woke up just as confused and forgetful as I could be. I'd purely forgotten what we'd talked about, young man, but now it's coming back ... slowly, slowly. Maybe I'd remember better if I had a bottle of stimulant."

"Forget the 'stimulant.' I want you sober this time."

"Ah, yes. Sobriety. A virtue, sobriety. Virtues are to be lauded, unlike evils ... evils such as, oh, poverty ..."

"You cussed devil," Ben said, surprising the fellow. Ben dug in his pocket and handed the man a coin. What little money he had was merely the remains of his meager pay as Cathedral overseer, and he had little to spare for drunks who might know nothing at all. "That's all the money you'll get from us, and if you have no information to provide, I'll beat you until you beg to give even that back. You savvy, friend?"

The man cocked his brows aristocratically. "Sir, you are a barbarian."

Andy said, "Talk, friend. What do you know about Deborah Bray?"

"Well, quite truthfully, I don't know that I know anything about this Bray woman, sir, in that I don't know the name of the woman I saw. Might you describe this Miss Bray?"

"I described her last night."

"Yes ... but perhaps a reminder ..."

Ben impatiently described Deborah Bray and her masculine disguise, the lively brows of his listener wiggling above brown eyes. "Oh, indeed, that is the very woman I saw!'' he said. ''But I can't be sure that the man I saw with her is the one you are after. Might you describe him, too?''

''I can't,'' Ben said. ''I've never seen him. But he would be roughly her age, not many years' difference.''

''Brown hair?''

''I don't know.''

''Well, sir, the man I saw had brown hair, a youngish appearance, well dressed and groomed.''

''And what was he doing?''

''He was with the young lady, speaking to her harshly. He seemed angry that she was dressed as she was. He grasped her arm. . . .''

''Did you hear any threats?''

''Threats? Why, yes. He was quite threatening. I couldn't understand his words, but he seemed to be threatening to carry her off somewhere.''

''Where?''

''I couldn't hear. But his manner disturbed me sufficiently to make me follow him and the lady some distance.''

''Wait . . . you *saw* him take her away?''

''I did.''

''And where did he take her?''

''To a cabin. Above the place where the pressure cannon work.''

''One of the old gold miner cabins?''

''Yes. One quite close to the rim of that sheer bluff left by the blasting of the water cannon. The one visible from the mountain road.''

''I know the place. And all this happened yesterday?''

''Indeed.''

''Andy, we have to get up there.''

''I know. If there's any point. He might have already . . .''

''Might have, but maybe not.''

The little man, looking from face to face, apparently realized that they were finished with him. He backed away, cautiously, then tipped his round little hat and scurried off.

"We've got to arm ourselves," Ben said.

"There's two rifles at the house. We'll get a couple. But I don't want my mother to see us do it. She'd not be happy to know what we're doing."

"I hope Deborah's alive. I hope she's all right."

They hurried back toward Jake's house, the little man watching them from an alley. When they went out of sight, he bit the coin Ben had given him, nodded his satisfaction, cocked his hat to one side, and scurried toward the nearest barroom.

They knelt behind a jumble of boulders, eyeing the little cabin.

"Don't look like there's been anybody there for a long time," Andy whispered.

"I know. But we'll have to get closer to be sure."

"Ben, do you think that little varmint was telling us the truth?"

"I don't know. It seemed believable while he was saying it."

"Ben, I ain't ever done anything like this. Have you?"

Through Ben's mind flashed images of himself, in the company of bushwhackers whom he hated but pretended to admire, creeping through wartime forests toward the unsuspecting homes of men soon destined to feel the sting of Henry Champion and his band. "Yes, I have. But it's been a long time."

"Maybe you should lead the way. You being experienced, and all."

"Maybe so."

But as Ben led the slow creep toward the cabin, he didn't feel experienced, or like a leader. He felt old and battered and ill-suited for such a grim task.

The cabin was small, but seemed to grow as they approached. Ben's mouth was dry, his hands trembling, causing him to grip his rifle tightly to hide it. He felt more like a foolish old man with every yard he advanced, and Andy seemed more a boy. And the mysterious, unseen Daniel

Bray seemed more demonic, a fearsome being Ben dreaded even to meet.

"Ben, you think they're in there?"

"I don't know. . . . Listen, Andy. This isn't your matter. There's no reason you should go any farther. What would I tell your father if something happened to you?"

"I'm coming with you," Andy said, trying but failing to sound brave.

Ben nodded. "All right. If you feel like you—"

He cut off quickly and dropped his face as Andy did the same. A terrible, explosive roar had erupted, making the very ground rumble and shake. A stinging white mist blasted up from somewhere just beyond the old cabin, raining back down upon them.

The water cannon had erupted into operation, grinding down the mountain a little farther as the last of the high country's gold miners manhandled the land with an effectiveness their dish-swishing predecessors could only have envied.

"Scared me nigh to death," Andy said, though Ben could no longer hear him. The cannon roar was far too loud and endless. Ben motioned for Andy to continue.

At least any sound they made in approaching would be masked.

Nearer they came, slowly creeping, eyes stinging in the fine spray bursting up from below the edge of the bluff, rifles growing wet in their grasps.

They reached the rear of the cabin. Ben sucked in a deep, moist breath and edged to the window. . . .

He gazed in for several seconds, rifle at the ready, eyes exploring the dark interior.

"What is it, Ben?" Andy asked. He went unheard.

Ben lifted a leg and put it through the empty window, then pulled the rest of himself through, vanishing from Andy's sight.

A minute later, both men stood inside the cabin, protected momentarily from the blasting mist. The roar of the water cannon was sufficiently muffled by the log walls to allow them to speak to one another. If the sound had suddenly shut down they would have discovered they were shouting at each other. As it was, they had to strain to hear what each other said.

"I should have known, Andy," Ben said. "I should have seen that shrimp was lying to us. He never saw a thing."

"But he said he saw her, even described what she was wearing."

"No, he didn't. *We* described it. We fed him everything he needed to know in the way we questioned him, and he just threw it right back to us. For the money."

Andy pondered and nodded. "We've been fools. Me the biggest of all. I'm the one who led us to that lying drunk."

"Well, in one way maybe it's all for the best. If he'd been telling the truth, most likely we'd have found her dead up here."

The cabin quaked and rumbled, the blasting sound growing louder as the cannon fired their jets at a point just below the top of the bluff.

"What now, Ben?"

"We get out of here and back to town. Then we keep looking, at least for a while. If you're willing, at least."

"And if we don't find her?"

"Then we go back to the mine, and start doing what miners are supposed to do."

"There's something I ain't mentioned to you about the mine, Ben. Something that happened the day of the night that Roscoe got burned up."

"What?"

"We hit a horse down in the shaft."

"You hit a *what*?"

"A horse . . . you know what I mean. A big block of iron. Seems to be right monstrous."

"So all that digging . . ."

"Has been for nothing."

The roaring was growing louder, the cabin beginning to shake and shiver, making strange, twisting, straining noises . . . but Ben was proccupied with what he'd just been told, and hardly noticed.

"But ain't there some way we can—"

He saw the look on Andy's face, the fear that rose suddenly in his eyes, the opening of the mouth to scream, but the scream was never heard. Something struck the cabin that felt like the very fist of God, slamming the base of it, ripping it asunder and pushing it up and back, the course suddenly reversing as the cabin, cut loose by a stray blast from one of the water cannon, now spilled out and down, pitching over the edge of the bluff and tumbling, turning, crashing down the slope into the white hell of water and stone below, carrying its two screaming human occupants with it.

Chapter Eighteen

Ben felt nothing. He was numb all over . . . no, not completely numb. There was cold. A chill that embraced him from head to foot. Wetness. And a shaking, ear-attacking, grumbling roar, like the growl of Satan angered.

Ben opened his eyes and saw a gray-white blur. All a jumble, nothing making sense, everything askew, twisted, bent at incredible angles. His focus came back, partially, and he saw Andy amidst it all, lying on his back. One leg was stretched out before him. The other was bent impossibly, as if he'd gained a new joint in the middle of his thigh. Andy didn't move. His eyes were closed.

Ben closed his eyes, too, and wondered if he had gone to hell. If so, all the usual tales were wrong. Hell was supposed to be hot, not cold and wet.

The roaring was gone, replaced by a steady, dull buzzing that seemed to come from inside his own head. No more cold, either. He was warm now, and lying on something soft. He opened his eyes again, and looked into a face, and blandly thought, *I was right. I have gone to hell.*

The man looking back at him was Henry Champion.

Odd that it should be Champion who came to welcome him to the infernal regions. Or maybe not. Maybe it was part of the torment of damnation that your most hated enemies became your eternal companions.

"Mr. Woolard, I'm so glad to see you awake," Henry Champion said in a voice that wasn't Henry Champion's. "We were quite worried about you."

Ben stared at the face. A gentle and smiling face. His mind cleared a bit, and now he knew. This wasn't Henry Champion at all. He'd made the same mistake that Roanie had. This was that newcomer preacher, the one who merely happened to resemble Champion.

"Am I alive?"

"Yes."

"So I've not gone to hell?"

The preacher gave him an odd look. "No. Oh, no. You're in your brother's house. You were found yesterday afternoon, almost dead, soaked and covered with dirt and rubble and gravel. You were at the place where the huge water cannons blast away the mountain. Do you remember?"

Ben felt his heart begin to race. "I remember."

"You wouldn't have survived much longer. It's astonishing that you survived as long as you did. Had you fallen facedown instead of on your back, you'd have drowned."

Another memory . . . "Andy. What about Andy?"

"Alive. A badly broken leg. But he seems well otherwise. And you, sir, are remarkably blessed. Not a single bone of your body broken."

"I hurt anyway."

"Well you should. It appears that you and the younger Mr. Woolard fell inside a cabin from the top of the bluff all the way to the base of the pit."

"That's exactly what happened."

"Why were you there?"

"First you tell me why you're here."

"They were afraid you'd die. They knew I was a minister of the gospel. Thus I was called in."

''Tell them I don't plan to die.''

''Gladly. Now, why were you in such a dangerous place?''

''Looking for somebody. A man named Daniel Bray.''

Silence for a moment. ''How odd.''

''Why odd?''

''Because, Mr. Woolard, you've found the man you were looking for. My name is Bray. The Reverend Daniel Bray, and I'm quite pleased to have the pleasure of your aquaintance.''

Ben gazed at the preacher for a long time, wondering if he'd really heard what he thought he'd heard. His head buzzed; he realized he'd probably been administered some sort painkiller before he fully regained consciousness.

''Did you say your name is Daniel Bray?''

''Yes.''

''You don't look as young as I thought you'd be.''

''Tell me, sir, how you had heard my name, and why you were looking for me.''

The buzzing in Ben's head grew louder. He didn't know what he should or shouldn't say to this man, but his tongue seemed loosened by whatever he'd been administered, and he spoke freely. ''I heard of you from Deborah Bray. Says she's your half sister. Says you murdered her father, your own father.''

He slowly shook his head. ''Oh, dear girl. My dear girl . . . so beautiful. So ill. So . . . destroyed.''

Ben wasn't in much shape or mood for talking, but this intrigued him. ''What do you mean, 'destroyed'?''

''Deborah isn't well, Mr. Woolard. She's ill. Not physically. Her mind.''

''Are you saying she's insane?''

Bray was slow to answer. He suddenly seemed older. ''I suppose that's what I am saying. But they're not easy words. Not for a father to say about his daughter.''

If Ben had felt like it, he would have sat up. ''Daughter? Deborah is your daughter?''

''Indeed she is. You see, Mr. Woolard, there is no half

157

brother named Daniel Bray. That's what she told you, I suppose—that she is fleeing from a wicked half brother named Daniel, that he committed some dread crime, that she has information that can lead to his downfall, and that he's after her, intent on killing her."

"That's what she told me. She said that Daniel killed her father . . . killed *you*."

"Mr. Woolard, I am the only Daniel Bray still alive. Daniel Bray my son—the twin brother of poor Deborah—died when he was eight years old. A terrible accident. Deborah saw it, the only one who did. I gave up years ago trying to determine the exact circumstances of his death. Deborah would never say . . . at least, she would never say the same thing twice. It involved fire, that much I can tell you. The poor boy, my son, burned to death in an abandoned house that he and Deborah had been playing in together."

"I'm sorry."

"Yes. In any case, when he died, he and I were at odds. Nothing important, just a case of his misbehavior and my punishment, and him holding resentment over it. I gather that he'd made comments about having bad intent toward me. Perhaps he said he'd kill me. . . . childish metaphor, if he did. No true intent. But Deborah seemed to believe he was serious. She believed he really wanted me hurt or dead."

"Reverend Bray, are you trying to hint that . . ."

"I'm trying to hint that it's possible that Deborah killed her own twin brother at the age of eight. Not certain. Possible. It took me years to be able to admit even the possibility. But suffice it to say that after Daniel's death, Deborah began a slow and continual slide into very dark places. Her sanity failed her. Her mother and I did all we could for her, sought her the best care and wisest men. She improved. She became very much a normal young woman, her perspective in the right place. Only when the matter of Daniel came up did she seem . . . abnormal. Unable to cope. And when her mother died, she lost everything she had gained, and more. She began talking as if Daniel had killed her. She claimed to have papers—just blank sheets of paper, nothing more—that proved he intended to kill me. And she would sometimes dress in a man's clothing, and claim that she was him.''

"Wait . . . she was in man's clothing when I met her. But she didn't claim to be Daniel. She claimed to be hiding from him, dressing that way to disguise herself.''

Bray shook his head. "No. Perhaps she was clever enough to use that story because it was more acceptable to others. But the fact is, she dresses in male clothing not to escape Daniel, but to *be* him. She and Daniel are one and the same, Mr. Woolard. One and the same.''

Ben was so caught up, so fascinated and appalled by all this, that he was hardly aware of his own injuries. "Mr. Bray, I need to tell you something. When I met Deborah, it was while I was operating a sort of hotel for my brother. Not really a hotel, just a big warehouse full of bunks where men, only men, could pay for a bed for a night. Deborah came in, dressed as a man, and to make a long story short, I realized she wasn't what she appeared.'' He quickly related his other condescensions to Deborah, and how Roscoe Hammel had treated her with equal protectiveness and liberality. Then he paused, and went on: "This sleeping house, sir, was destroyed very recently by fire. On a night Deborah was sleeping there. And afterward she told me that she saw Daniel do it.''

The old reverend went pale, and sat weakly down in a chair beside Ben's bed. So far none of Ben and Andy's kin had come into the closed room, and for this Ben was glad, because only in privacy could such a delicate and informative conversation as this one proceed.

"Oh, Mr. Woolard, it pains me to hear that. She set it, then. Deborah set that fire.'' He squeezed his eyes tightly closed a few seconds, pursing his lips. Then he looked at Ben again. "Did anyone die?''

"One man.''

"God help us. God help us.''

"I'm sorry to have told you that.''

"Mr. Woolard, don't be sorry. It's providential that we

met, you and I. I mean that literally. Our meeting was intended, because through you I've found my daughter's track at last, and learned things, however painful, that I needed to know.''

"And so have I, sir. I believed Deborah's story. She's quite persuasive.''

"Of course. After all, she believes it herself.''

"Is there any hope for her? Can she ever be sane?''

"I don't know. Perhaps. There are those years of lucidity that she enjoyed. Those give me hope. Maybe she can return to them, and this time not lose touch again.'' He paused. "But this death, this fire . . . that makes it all different. If she's responsible for a man's death . . .''

"Sir, if you would, say nothing to anyone about that. The fact is that we don't know that she set the fire. Maybe someone else did set it, and she saw them, and in her state of mind interpreted that person as her half brother.''

Bray, obviously eager for any hope he could find, seized on that idea eagerly. "Yes! Yes! Perhaps so. I'll assume the best for now, for Deborah's sake.''

"You must know, sir, that I haven't seen Deborah since the night of that fire. That's why Andy and I were looking for Daniel Bray—the imagined one, not you. We thought he'd found her and taken her off. In fact, we met a man, a town drunk, who swore to us that he'd seen a woman who sounded like Deborah being carried off by a young man.''

"Mercy! Might he really have seen something, somebody taking her away?''

"No. I'm convinced he didn't. Andy and I went about questioning this fellow in entirely the wrong way. We fed him his answers in the very questions we asked, and he gave us back what we seemed to be looking for so that we'd pay him. He lied to us for money, told us we'd find the people he saw up in that cabin above the rock pit. But when we got inside, it was obvious that no one had been in that place for years.''

"So Deborah is still missing.''

"Yes. Perhaps she's gone on elsewhere, sir.''

"Perhaps. She travels far. I've been trying to find her

for a year now. A full year, following rumors, tracing down clues about her whereabouts. . . . It's hard. Terribly hard.''

"Maybe she's still in town. Maybe we can find her. There's new people streaming into Ferguson every day, Reverend. Huge crowds of folks. A person can lose themselves in such a town with ease.''

Reverend Bray bowed his head, and Ben wondered if he was praying. But when he lifted his face again, his eyes were red and wet. The weary, worried man had been crying. Weeping for a missing, insane daughter who might have once more slipped out of his reach.

If Ben had any doubts about the veracity of Bray's tale, he let them go at that point. At times all that could be trusted were instincts. He believed Bray. Everything about him had the aura of authenticity.

"I'll help you search for her, Reverend. I'd consider it a privilege.''

"I don't think you're in much shape to help just now, my friend.''

"You'll be surprised. I've come through two beatings already, and I'm not out yet. If I can do that, and then slide down a mountain and come out without a single broken bone, then I believe I can do most anything. I'll be up and about in no time, and you and me will find your daughter, sir.''

Bray smiled and nodded. "God bless you, Mr. Woolard. You are a saint.''

"No. I just sense your concern for her. You care about her. And so do I.''

Bray stood. "Mr. Woolard, I've done you a disservice. Here I've been brought in to sit with you and pray over you until you awakened, and now that you have, all I've done is chatter on about my own situation. Your brother doesn't even know that you've come back to the living!''

"Then maybe you can go tell them.''

Bray nodded, smiling more firmly. "That I shall. And thank you, sir. Thank you for your pledge to help me.''

"Not at all.''

Ben settled back into the pillow as Bray left the room, and waited for the others to come to him.

Chapter Nineteen

Andy was quite jealous. With his painful broken leg, splinted and bound and propped up before him, he would be abed for heaven only knew how long. And yet Ben, merely a week after that tumble over the bluff and not that much farther past the second of two beatings, was already up and about and doing quite well.

Not bad for a man working through his fifth decade of life. Andy could only lie as still as possible, and envy him.

He had other things to think about, too. Like his father's odd manner. For the last three days, Jake Woolard had seemed very distracted, not himself at all. Something was on the man's mind, heavily so, but he denied it each time Andy asked him about it.

At the moment, Andy was fairly comfortable, but it wouldn't last. The doctor was scheduled to stop by later in the day, and, as usual, he'd poke and prod about at that broken leg until it was so sore Andy wanted to weep. Then he'd tell Andy to remain still, leave the leg alone, and wait for him to come back in a day or two and torture him some more.

Andy closed his eyes and decided to nap. If he could. Laid up in bed, about all a man could do was nap, and after so much sleep, more of the same wasn't much appealing.

Andy drew in a deep breath, moved a little to resettle himself—wincing at the pain this caused to shoot through his leg—and vowed never again to join Ben Woolard on any quest for any woman or any mysterious stranger.

Once he was out of this bed, Andy Woolard would return to mining and be glad to have no further adventures.

Ben rocked slowly on the porch, looking out into the evening, when the door opened behind him and Jake emerged.

"Well, howdy, Ben. I didn't realize you were out here."

"I don't have to be, if you were looking for some privacy. I can go back inside."

"Oh, no, sit still." He pulled up the other rocker. "What makes you think I'd want you to go away?"

"Maybe the fact that you've had a kind of distant manner about you this week."

"Have I?"

"Yes. Andy and me were talking about it only today. And Sally has mentioned it more than once. I think she's worried about you." Ben paused. "I am, too. It isn't like you to act like this. Is something wrong at the store?"

"No. Everything's fine at the store."

"But something's wrong somewhere. Right?"

A moment of silence, then Jake looked over at his brother. "Ben, I saw Henry Champion."

"What?"

"I saw him. The day after you and Andy went over the cliff in the cabin. I saw him standing in the doorway of a saloon, looking across the street at me. He was in the shadows, and I don't think he realized I could see him . . . but it was him. Not the preacher Bray, either. There was no mistake this time."

Ben felt tense all over. "Jake, could it really be that somehow the man really is alive?"

"It has to be. I know because I saw him."

"We saw him hang, too."

"But maybe we didn't see him die."

"Surviving a military hanging? No. Can't be. You heard the sound when that rope jerked tight. You could feel the force of that snap when he hit the end of that rope. A jerk like that would break any man's neck. He couldn't have made it through alive. And if he had, wouldn't it have been known right away?"

"I can't explain. All I know is what I saw. And that I'm scared by it. He was looking at me, Ben. Right at me! Staring with those same cold eyes that I felt on me when I was testifying in his trial."

"I don't know what to say."

"Neither do I. Just be sure to keep that pistol I gave you with you all the time."

"I will. You stay armed, too. Just in case." He thought about it some more and shook his head. "Jake, he *can't* be alive! It isn't possible."

"I saw him, Ben. I saw him just like that colored man said he saw him."

"Roanie . . . And you know something, Jake? Roanie hasn't been around lately. I haven't seen him, anyway."

"Maybe Champion got him."

"I'd just as soon you not say that kind of thing. Makes me nervous."

"Ben, there's more to it than me just seeing Champion, as if that wasn't enough. I did some investigation. I found out that there's a mining claim in the Goatbeard area held by a man named Marcus Fellers."

"Fellers . . . good Lord, Jake. Ain't that the name that Jim Masker used for himself from time to time?"

"It is. Maybe it's coincidence, but a mighty odd one if it is. And from what I was able to find out by asking around among the miners I know from around Goatbeard, this Fellers man matches the looks of Jim Masker, and there's men with him, some of whom sound like they might be Champion and Art Rellon. And a couple of younger men, too, apparently grown-up sons of the others."

"Jake, this scares me to death."

165

"Don't it, though."

Ben rocked a few moments more. "I think I might go inside now, Jake. All at once I don't feel too safe sitting out here."

"I'll join you."

They rose and entered the house, seeking the shelter of protective walls in a night that suddenly seemed more than a little ominous.

Ben spent the next day with Reverend Bray, searching the town for Deborah. Bray was intense and focused on his quest, talking only of what they were doing at the moment, unable to know that when his still-limping companion cut his eyes here and there to examine the throngs of Ferguson, it was not only for Deborah Bray that he looked.

The aging preacher began the day full of hope that he would find his daughter, and it was sad to watch his spirits declining as the day waned. "We'll find her tomorrow," Ben said as brightly as possible.

"Can we not continue to look a bit longer?" Reverend Bray pleaded. "Just a bit more? The night brings out more people in a town like this one."

Ben was tired, increasingly suspicious that Deborah had already left Ferguson entirely, probably fleeing because somewhere in her troubled mind she knew that it wasn't any phantom half brother, but she herself, who had burned down the Cathedral. And there was something else nagging at Ben, too, a feeling that he needed to return to Jake's house, that it was very important that he be there very soon.

But the old preacher's sad, pleading face was hard to deny. "A while longer," Ben said. "Just a half hour or so. Maybe we'll find her after all."

"I'm sure of it!" Bray said, suddenly bright and full of life. "Thank you, sir! You are indeed a godsend to me."

And so they searched on, but no Deborah was found. And the unsettled feeling that had plagued Ben, calling him vainly back to Jake's house, only grew. At last he could continue no more, and told the preacher that he'd now be heading back but would be ready to continue the search the next day.

Ben set out toward Jake's house on a trot, and was almost there when a small boy intercepted him. "Mr. Woolard, sir? Mr. Ben Woolard?"

"Yes."

"I got something for you. A message."

"Who from?"

"I don't know. Just a man who gave me two dollars to watch for you and make sure you got it." He handed Ben a folded piece of paper, sealed with wax, then waited expectantly. Ben sighed and reached into his pocket and handed the boy a coin. He was completely out of money now, relying on handouts from Jake to get him by, and he didn't like parting with even a small amount of cash. The boy grinned and trotted away with his money.

Ben unfolded the paper and read. Wadding it, he crammed it into a pocket, turned, and ran back up Center Street as hard as his bruised and tired body would allow.

He found the store locked and dark except for a single light burning back in the storeroom, where Jake kept a desk upon which he worked through the store's books and ledgers each evening.

"Jake!" Ben yelled, pounding the door with his fist. "Jake! Are you in there?"

Jake appeared in the storeroom door, frowning and gazing across the dark store interior toward whatever maniac was pounding down his front door. "Ben? Is that you?"

"Let me in, Jake!"

Jake hurried across the store and admitted Ben. "What the devil is wrong?"

"Nothing, it appears. But I got a note on the street—a boy handed it to me—and it said you were in here, hurt and bleeding, and that you'd be dead by the time I found you."

"What? Ben, I'm fine, as you can see. Nothing's happened to me."

167

"I know. I can see that. Either this is some kind of a joke . . . or a warning . . ."

Jake looked solemn. "Or maybe an attempt to keep you from going where you were going at the time. Where were you heading when you met this boy?"

"To the house. Your house."

A pause. "Ben, let's go. Let's go now."

They left the store together, not even pausing to shut the door behind them, and ran hard up the street, through the milling and half-drunken crowd, toward Jake's house.

Andy had tried to fight them, impossible though it was. He'd somehow dragged himself out of his bed and gone for one of his father's rifles in the rifle case, but someone had gotten to him long before it was within reach, and pounded him senseless with the butt of a shotgun. He lay now with his bleeding head cradled in the lap of his weeping mother. She was bleeding too, shot through the shoulder, and her nose was broken and dripping scarlet liquid that washed over her lips and fell onto her son's pale face.

Jake all but fell before her, groping out, weeping, asking her what had happened, and who . . .

"They got Judy," she said. "They got Judy, they took her. They took her, Jake!"

"Who was it, Sally?" Ben asked urgently.

"I don't know . . . men. . . . They left a letter with your name on it, Jake."

"Where?"

Ben had already spotted it, lying on the supper table. "Here it is." He grabbed it, handed it to his brother.

Jake shook his head. "My hands are trembling too much. Open it, Ben. Read it."

Ben's hands were almost as tremulous, but he managed to get the envelope open and the paper spread. He read it silently, then read it again.

"Champion?" Jake asked.

Ben nodded and let the paper fall from his fingers.

"He wants us?"

"Yes. If we want to see Judy alive again, he says, we

have to come to him, to his claim at Goatbeard. For a 'reckoning.' That's what it says. A 'reckoning.' And we have to come alone, and unarmed. Any weapons, any law in sight, and he'll kill her.''

Sally sobbed, out of control. Andy groaned and moved, an encouraging sign, but hardly noticed under the circumstances.

''We've got to do it, Ben.''

''I know.''

Sally screamed, ''No, Jake! They'll kill you! I saw them, I know what kind of men they are. . . . They'll kill you!''

''I have to do it, honey. For Judy.''

Sally leaned across her unconscious son and wept like a child.

Chapter Twenty

Funny, Ben thought, how there seemed nothing to say. Two brothers, walking alone in the night along a trail that would lead to their deaths at the hands of a man long believed dead—and there was nothing to say. He and Jake strode side by side, looking straight ahead, walking unarmed and unfollowed into the night, and neither had a word to say to the other.

Though the night was quite dark, the trail was relatively easy to keep to once their eyes fully adjusted. Many a miner traveled the route between Ferguson and Goatbeard day after day, and footfalls and hoofbeats and wagon wheels had made a road of what had once been untrampled mountain soil.

They strode on, ever silent.

They saw the fire, just as promised, a bonfire flickering below the overhang of Goatbeard. They made for it. A beacon to guide them, put there by Champion and his cohorts. A beacon to lure two men to their deaths . . . and yet they had no option but to follow, because of Judy.

Jake stopped, turned, and looked behind them. "Did you hear that?"

"No," Ben said. "What was it?"

"It sounded like someone following."

"I didn't hear."

"I hope no one followed. My God, what will they do to Judy if someone followed, and they detect it?"

Ben listened hard. "Jake, there's no one back there. I think you imagined it."

Jake shook his head. "I heard something."

"A critter, probably. Now let's move on. If we're late, Judy might pay the price."

They trudged up the mountain, toward the flickering light.

Art Rellon was the first person they saw. They were close enough to the bonfire now to make out the figures of men around it, and Art Rellon was suddenly before them, stepping out onto the trail with a shotgun in hand.

"Ben Woolard!" he said in an oddly warm voice. "So that really was you I met on the street a while back! Who'd have thought we'd wind up in the same town!"

"Where is she, Rellon?"

"The girl? Why, she's fine. Henry's got her."

Jake spoke. "If he lays a hand on her to harm her or to shame her in any way, I'll slice him into pieces, a little at a time."

Rellon laughed. "My Lord, ain't you two the somber ones? What's wrong? You afraid somebody's going to betray you? Put you into a situation that endangers your life? Is that it?" He paused. "I guess you're pretty much an expert when it comes to betraying folks, eh, Ben?"

"Where's Judy? When will you let her go?"

"Ain't up to me. It's up to Henry." Rellon laughed. "I'll bet that strikes you odd, hearing talk about Henry, when you've thought him dead for so damn long!"

"Henry Champion can have me, as long as he lets Judy go," Ben said. "And there's no reason he should want to harm my brother. It was me who put him on the gallows."

"Your brother played his part, too. I do believe it was him you reported back to, betraying Henry, betraying all of

172

us, all that time you were pretending to be one of us." He waved the shotgun. "Now come on. Let's let you go say hello to an old friend."

Ben was sure that at any moment he would open his eyes and find himself staring at Jake's ceiling. Maybe even the ceiling of the Cathedral, with all that had occurred in the last few days proving to be no more than a bizarre dream.

But every time he closed and reopened his eyes, the same vision was before him: Henry Champion, alive and in the flesh, standing beside the bonfire with a rope in his hand, the other end of which was tied around Judy Woolard's plump neck.

The murderous old bushwhacker had her leashed like some dog! Ben felt his blood surge hot. He wondered if there was some symbolic significance to the rope being around her neck—a subtle reminder that he was Henry Champion, the gallowsman who had somehow managed to survive his own hanging. Was he hinting that the Woolard brothers were going to be forced to watch a mere child hanged as punishment for their long-past offense?

Henry Champion looked Jake up and down, then turned a far more lingering gaze upon Ben. He evaluated him silently, eyes trailing his entire form, expression never changing. In fact, Champion seemed to have no expression at all, just a chilling, unrelenting gaze.

"Hello, Ben," he said at last. "Last time I seen you, I was about to have a hanging mask pulled down over my face."

"How'd you live through it, Champion?" Ben asked. "I saw you drop. I saw the rope jerk tight around your neck."

Champion smiled for the first time. His smile had always made Ben shudder back in the old days. It was no different now. "What you think you see and what really happens ain't always the same thing. I did drop. I did jerk that rope tight. But it wasn't my neck that took the impact of it. There was a harness around me, under my arms, with a sort of hook on it. That rope was linked to that harness, so that when it pulled tight, I took the force of it around the chest, not the neck. God, that hurt, but damned better it was than the alternative. All I had to do was hang there limp and play dead.''

"Wait a minute . . . are you telling me that your hanging was a hoax?''

"I'm standing alive before you, ain't I?''

"But that would require the complicity of the Federals. . . . Somebody defied the order of the court.''

"My, my, ain't you just as smart as you ever was! You got it just right, Ben. There was complicity. Several layers of it, matter of fact. You see, even the Yankees had some among them who knew that it wasn't just for a man like me to hang when others who'd done as much or more than I had had been pardoned. There was several in that courtroom who knew, even while I was being sentenced to hang, that it would never happen. There was a plan to fake the thing almost from the time the sentence was read. When I mounted that gallows, I knew I'd be coming off it alive again.''

Ben had nothing to say. He'd never have believed such a thing as Champion was describing could have happened . . . but the evidence stood alive before him. His own government, his own side, illegitimately sparing the life of the man he'd risked his life to bring down. Suddenly Ben understood what it must have felt like to Henry Champion to see someone he'd trusted testifying against him in trial. The very Federal justice structure that Ben had aided and trusted without question had betrayed him.

"So you've been alive all these years.''

"That's right. Alive and kicking. Oh, I laid plenty low for many a year, and traveled many a mile. Came west eventually, using this name and that. I was a sodbuster for a time, and a rancher. I've been a merchant and a horse trader. Now I'm a miner. But all the while I've done what I could for the old cause. I've wore the white sheet and the white hood with pride. I've done my share to let Mister Nigger know that, free or not, he's still Mister Nigger, and I'm still his better.''

"It was you who killed Billy Platt.''

174

"Who's Billy Platt?"

"A Negro. Murdered and his teeth pulled out."

"That gold-mouth nigger! Oh, yes, that was my doing." Champion laughed, but quickly turned his look very hard and sour. "Damned nigger, going around flashing them gold teeth, thinking himself fine because of it! Damn, but it made my blood boil inside me! I reckon old gold-teeth had a different attitude by the time I finished with him! That was one nigger I particular enjoyed killing."

"You've killed a lot of men, Champion. Men who didn't deserve it. Even boys."

"I have. And I ain't through killing yet."

Ben glanced at Judy, who was biting her lip, crying, but doing her best to be brave. "You ain't going to stoop to hurting a little girl, are you?"

"I don't quite know what I'm going to do with this girl," he said, giving the rope a small jerk. "I believe I'll keep her close by for now, just to make sure you Woolards have good reason to cooperate."

Jake spoke. "We'll do whatever you say ... but please, please, let my girl go. Don't hurt her. I beg you."

"You beg me, do you? You beg me. If I'd begged for my life on them gallows, would you have felt bad for me? Would you have listened? Hell, no."

"Let's get on with it, Henry," Masker said.

"Let's do," Champion said. "Here. Come take this little gal's rope. Take her and tie her to a tree over yonder."

Masker led Judy off her head turning as she walked so she could maintain eye contact with her father. Masker tied his end of the rope tightly around a tree, then aimed a finger at Judy's face. "You try to get loose, and you'll regret it, girl!"

Champion walked slowly to Ben and looked him in the eye. For a long time he said nothing, then slowly he shook his head.

"Ben Woolard. Good Ben Woolard, who rode with me, told me time and again he supported what I believed in, what I did, what I was. You know, Ben, I trusted you. I took you at your word. You were like a son to me. I swear it's true. Like a son.''

"You were a murderer, Champion. A murderer then, and a murderer now.''

"I was a faithful, true son of the South. A man who knew the rightful scheme of the world and wasn't willing to let a bunch of niggers and nigger-loving bluebellies mess it all up. And I was a man who paid an eye for an eye. That's all I was.''

Ben said, "I'm not sorry for what I did. I've been proud of it all these years. I was proud that evidence I gathered was what convicted you, and proud that it was me who brought you to the noose.''

Champion actually looked sad. "Them words hurt, son. They do. I wish you'd been true to me. I wish you'd been what I thought you was.''

"Let me go, Champion. You'll gain nothing by doing harm to me now. And whatever you do, please, I beg you to let Judy there, and my brother here, come to no harm. Please.''

Champion made no promises. It was as if he didn't even hear. "It hurt me bad, seeing you Judas me like you did, son. Every word you said in that court, every word burned me like a brand.

"But I didn't carry my grudge against you close to my heart. No, sir. I could have sought you out in secret when it was all over, or could have had any one of these faithful men of mine do it, but I didn't. I let it be. Let you be. But then, when it begun to come clear that fate had brung us together once more, then I knew that justice had to be done.

"I didn't believe it at first. Here comes Rellon saying he'd seen you in town, face-to-face. I didn't believe it. Then Masker tells me he seen you, too, and that the Woolard who runs the mercantile was none other than your brother. Still I didn't quite believe, not until the day I seen you with my own eyes in a saloon in town, staring at a bottle you never touched.''

"You were there?''

"I was. I watched you and the young fellow with you.

When you were gone, I even took your bottle. And I drunk it, and thought, and drunk it some more, and thought some more, until I knew what had to be done. The old score had to be settled. And settled it'll be. Right here. Tonight."

Champion waved back across his claim. A typical kind of operation, not much different in looks than the one Ben, Andy, and Roscoe had worked. A pen with a couple of mules, a rough log storage shed for tools, heaps of dirt and stone, and a shaft with a wooden pulley frame—a "gallows," ironically—built atop it. And Champion's men, faces from Ben's past, and two younger men he knew were sons, though of which men he couldn't know. Ben took it all in with a sweep of his eyes, and felt sad to know that this would be the last scene he would ever see.

"Time for reckoning, son," he said. "I'm sorry it's come down to it." With that he wheeled quickly toward Jake, drew a heavy, ancient pistol, and swung it hard, smashing it into Jake's jaw, breaking open the flesh, knocking Jake cold in a bleeding, collapsing heap.

Judy screamed and began to sob. Rellon turned and cursed at her, told her to shut up, and she somehow managed to stifle the sounds of her weeping, though the weeping went on.

Champion reholstered the pistol. "We'll deal with him later," he said. "You're the one who matters most, Ben. You're the one who dies first."

Chapter Twenty-one

The horse was big and black. Champion's own and quite a prized beast, Ben was told. Ben sat astride it now. No saddle, just the horse between his legs, his hands tied behind his back, and a noose around his neck.

Champion stood to his side, looking up at him with that same sad expression, like a father sorrowful to see a wayward son bearing the cost of his own ill decisions.

"I'm awful sorry, Ben," he said. "What makes it even harder for me is knowing how you'll suffer. Not enough height to give any drop to the rope, so I guess you'll just have to choke it out. God have mercy on you, son."

"I wonder what God thinks, hearing the voice of a man like you calling his name," Ben replied. He was determined to meet his end with all the dignity and defiance he could muster.

"Why don't you ask him when you see him, which won't be long now," Champion replied.

Ben could no longer look at the man. He lifted his eyes and took a final look at his brother, still crumpled unconscious on the ground, then up to where Judy was tied . . .

179

. . . and he began to smile.

Champion saw it, and his eyes narrowed. "What are you smiling at, son? This ain't no time for smiling. You ought to be praying."

The smile lingered. It wasn't forced. What Ben had seen caused it to well up from inside, and he couldn't stop it if he tried.

Masker, off behind Champion, glared at Ben's grinning face, then turned to see what he was looking at.

"Henry . . . look."

"What?"

"She's gone, Henry. The girl is gone."

"What the hell . . ."

Champion looked. Masker was right. The rope that had held Judy Woolard bound was still tied to the tree, but Judy was gone. Champion swore and turned to Ben again.

"Where'd she go? How'd she get away?"

Ben smiled down at Champion. "Maybe a ghost got her loose. Maybe the phantoms of all the men and boys you murdered gathered and swooped down out of the sky and set her free."

"Damn you, answer me straight! What happened to her!"

"Looks to me like somebody cut her loose. Now, don't that give you cause to ponder! Somebody out there . . . somebody to witness what you're doing here, somebody to testify about it in court."

Champion tried to hide it, but fear came over him then. His eyes shot fire at Ben, and he turned to his men.

Masker spoke. "Henry, even if there ain't nobody else, and she just wiggled loose, she could still tell what happened."

"Get out there," he said. "Find that girl, and if there's anybody else about, find them too. Now!"

Every man scurried to respond. Henry Champion was still an unquestioned leader after all these years.

"Wait, Jim," Champion said to Masker. "You stay here with me. I want two of us guarding in case that one on the ground begins to wake up."

Masker seemed glad to oblige. Ben, who just kept on grinning, could understand the feeling. There was something quite ominous about that dark forest, a sense of a presence there that was almost diabolical, like the great Goatbeard peak itself had come to life and moved monstrously and vengefully in the blackness.

"Maybe the night is going to swallow them alive," Ben said to Champion. "Maybe all the wickedness you've done has come to life. Maybe it's hungry for the flesh of bad men."

"Shut up!" Champion bellowed.

"Let's hang him now," Masker said. "Just slap the horse out from under him and shut him up for good!"

"Not until I have that girl back. Not until I know there's no witnesses out there."

They heard a sound in the forest, an odd, gurgling noise. A human sound, it seemed. And then a soft, muffled thud.

"That's one," Ben said. "One gone. I wonder which. Rellon? I'll bet it was Rellon."

Champion aimed his finger up at Ben. "Damn you, Ben, if you keep that up, I *will* go ahead and move this horse. You understand me?"

Ben kept up the smile. Champion glared at him, and Masker's look was one of dark and pure hatred.

Another noise—a faint, masculine grunt, perhaps a muffled cry. Another soft thudding sound, like a heavy bag of grain being dropped as quietly as possible on the ground.

"That's two," Ben whispered, and Champion cursed at him again and made as if to slap the horse from beneath him. But he didn't. And Ben knew he wouldn't, not until he knew for sure that he could commit this murder without being witnessed by hostile eyes. Champion, for all his talk, all his power over others of his ilk, all his attempts to justify himself for his crimes, was at heart a coward. Surrounded by protection, he would act. Alone, he would falter.

Time passed. The horse fidgeted but did not move out from beneath Ben.

He kept on grinning. By heaven, he'd still be grinning when they pulled the horse from beneath him, if it came to that. He'd not give Champion the satisfaction of seeing him whimper or cringe from death.

More sounds from the forest, more silences. Then more noises, men falling in a silent battle. One of the sounds this time was a very distinct cry of pain. One of the younger men, Ben thought.

"I believe that's all of them, Champion," Ben said.

"You brought someone with you," Champion said. "After what I ordered, you had somebody follow!"

"No. We didn't. We followed your orders, told no one. But I believe maybe somebody has followed us anyway. Somebody has followed us all on their own."

"I'll kill you!"

"No you won't. Not until you know you can do it without being seen. You only kill in the dark, Champion. Men who you'd never face in the light, and never face alone. You're a coward. You've always been a coward."

"We'll see how brave *you* are, Ben, when you feel that horse move out from under you." Champion turned to Masker. "Jim, maybe you'd best get out there and see what's going on."

"What?"

"You heard me."

"You think I'm going out there? There's something out there, Henry. Somebody."

By the light of the bonfire, Ben saw Henry Champion's face go crimson. Champion opened his mouth to reply to Masker, but before he could speak, another voice did.

From the darkness.

"Henry Champion!"

Ben, still smiling, watched the ruddy face of a moment before suddenly go white.

"Somebody's calling you, Henry," he whispered.

"God . . ." Masker said, backing away. "God, Henry, that voice don't even sound human!"

Champion's lips moved, but his ability to speak seemed to have escaped him.

"Henry Champion!" the phantom voice called again. "Time for you to pay the price!"

Ben watched pure panic envelop two men. Champion's mouth moved silently, like a fish's. Masker wasn't trying to speak, but he backed away, looking wildly around, clearly unsure what to do, where to run. . . .

A shot erupted out in the darkness. Masker yelled. Blood spurted from a hole that suddenly appeared in his belly. He doubled forward, gripping his middle, making high noises in his throat.

The horse moved a little beneath Ben. His smile faded.

The second shot caught Masker in the top of the head and drove him back. He hit the ground dead, just as the horse spooked and ran forward, pulling out from beneath Ben. As the rope squeezed incredibly tight around his neck, Ben saw Champion run out of the clearing and into the forest, away from where the shots had come.

And then the pain became too great, the choking too intense, and Ben felt his consciousness begin to fade, his feet kicking wildly, his hands struggling with bonds that would not give, and his neck burning, stretching, constricting, unable to pull in air, unable to do anything but hurt like nothing had ever hurt him before.

The bonfire flickered brightly, shooting sparks to the sky. Then, in Ben's eyes, it began to grow faint, the flame losing its brilliance, dying away with his consciousness, fading toward nonentity like the spark of life inside him.

Jake Woolard opened his eyes and found himself gazing into the fire. His face hurt, and felt wet and warm. He tried to move and found it difficult, but a second effort succeeded and he sat up slowly. He touched his face, grimaced, and pulled in a sharp breath.

His face was laid open and bloody; he fancied that he had just touched his bare jawbone, exposed in the midst of the wound.

He looked at the fire, trying to think, and his eyes drifted to a rope tied to a tree.

He remembered, and came to his feet. Miraculously, he did not fall. "Judy," he said. "Judy."

But Judy was not there. He looked around the clearing.

No one was there. Not Champion, not any of his men. . . . And where was Ben?

There, on the ground. Lying flat on his face, unmoving, with a rope around his neck. Jake stared. "Ben?" His eyes drifted up and saw the other portion of the rope still hanging from the limb above Ben. It appeared that Ben had been hanged, and the rope cut while he was still swinging.

Jake stumbled toward his brother and fell to his knees beside him. "Ben, are you alive?"

He touched him. The flesh felt warm. He pressed Ben's shoulder.

A groan. Ben was alive.

"I'm going to roll you over, Ben. Going to roll you over so you can breathe. . . ."

It took almost all his strength to do it. Ben was limp and unhelpful in the effort, a deadweight sack of flesh and bone that almost struggled against him. Even so, in a few moments Jake had him on his back.

After that he just stared at Ben's face, watching him suck in air, watching him gradually come to life again, like some sunken swimmer slowly rising to the surface of the water.

Ben opened his eyes.

"Ben, it's me. It's Jake. They hanged you, Ben. But somebody must have cut you down."

Ben groaned again.

"It wasn't me who did it. I was out cold . . . you were already on the ground when I came to. Ben, where's Judy? Where did they take her? Where's my daughter?"

Ben seemed to be trying to speak, but his throat was damaged. He had no voice.

"Can you stand, Ben? Do you have the strength?"

Ben managed to nod.

"I'll help you . . . we'll go back to town, get help. Come back and find Judy. Got to find Judy."

Rising was difficult for Ben, and when at last he was on his feet he wasn't sure he could remain there. But with his bleeding, gash-faced brother serving as a human crutch at his side, Ben managed to take one step, then another. On and on, over and over, until they were in the dark forest, heading along the trail toward town.

"Who did it, Ben? Who cut you down?"

Ben tried to answer, but still that crushed throat was unable to produce sound.

They walked on, hurting and weak, but growing stronger in the effort. They would make it. Reach Ferguson, and find help.

And somehow, they would find Judy. Somehow.

They did find her, without even trying.

Moving along the street, two battered brothers, they attracted much attention from Ferguson's nocturnal populace. Crowds of gaping men parted like water before a ship's prow as the pair moved along, holding each other up, heading for Jake's house. Jake talked to those around him, urging them to help him find his girl, babbling on about old Civil War bushwhackers and lynchings and men who were supposed to be dead but weren't, and no one paid heed because they couldn't make sense of it.

They continued down the street together, and when they neared the place where the Cathedral had stood, Ben saw something that stunned him so that his voice, or a part of it, stirred to life again.

"Jake . . . it's Judy." A coarse, soft whisper, but Jake heard it and understood.

"Where, Ben?"

"There," he whispered, and pointed.

And indeed she was there, weeping and terrified, seated in the lap of a woman who held her close and caressed her gently. An angel, she appeared in the eyes of the two men. A kind angel, comforting a girl who had been through an ordeal no girl should have ever had to face.

Judy saw her father, and the tears abruptly stopped. She stared at him, saw the wound, and for a moment her expression was impossible to read. Then she wailed out again, left the lap of the comforting woman, and ran to her father, throwing her arms around him and sobbing against his chest.

"There, girl, there now," Jake said. "It's all right, dear heart. It's all right."

Ben, leaving Jake with his daughter, walked slowly toward the woman, who stood to meet him. She was a pretty woman, hair unkempt but beautiful nonetheless, dress tattered and a little large, yet flattering and feminine. Her gaze was unblinking and firm.

It took Ben several moments to comprehend that he was looking into the face of Deborah Bray.

Chapter Twenty-two

It was after midnight. Judy sat alone by the stove, on her stool, a plate of food in her lap. Untouched. Not a bite had been eaten, and her stare had hardly broken from the opposite wall in the last fifteen minutes. She'd asked to be left alone, and her wish had been granted, though they had to nearly tear her mother away from her. Sally Woolard slept now, having taken an opiate to calm her ragged and ruined nerves. Jake, his face now stitched back together, slept beside her, similarly drugged. Andy was no longer in the house. He'd been taken off by the doctor to be placed in a bed at the doctor's private little ward, where he could be watched. But prospects looked good for him. He was expected to recover.

Ben walked in slowly and looked at Judy. Her eyes drifted over and met his. He advanced and sat down slowly in a chair near her.

"I know you want to be alone, but you and me need to talk," he said. His voice was still a whisper and would remain so for a long time, until the rope bruise healed. "About what happened out there. And the person who helped you."

"Did you see him, Uncle Ben?" Her voice was a whisper, too, but he did not know if this was because she was unconsciously mimicking him or because she sensed the need for confidentiality.

"No. Just a shadow of movement, that's all. But I think I know who it was. I heard his voice later, when he called out to Henry Champion. Did you hear that?"

"No. I was running then. That's what he told me to do. He cut me free, carried me off on his shoulder, away from that place, and set me down on the trail. He pointed his finger and told me the way to go. And he told me to run. It was hard to see him well in the dark, because his skin was—"

"No, Judy, don't tell me that. It's best I don't really know. That way, if there are questions, I don't have to lie. I don't want you to tell me any more about how he looked, what kind of man he was, anything like that. Do you understand why I don't want to know?"

"No."

"Because this man, if he's who I think he is, is a good man, but he could be in trouble if it was found out what he did."

"Because he let me go?"

"No. Because of what he did after that."

"What did he do, Uncle Ben?"

Ben hesitated; this did not seem the kind of thing to be telling a child. "He . . . destroyed them. He killed them."

"All of them?"

"I don't know. I only saw one of them actually die. A man who was shot in the clearing, from out of the darkness."

"I heard the shots. While I was running."

"But I think he killed others, too. Champion, the leader, sent his men out into the dark to find him, but he found them instead. I believe that when morning comes, the law will explore that claim and the area around it, and I believe they'll find the bodies."

"Did the man in the dark kill the leader?"

"I don't know. Champion ran away, out of the clearing,

away from where the others had gone, and from where the shots had come. I don't know what happened to him after that.''

''Are you going to tell the law people about the dead men, Uncle Ben?''

''I've been thinking about that, Judy, and I don't think I will. I don't want to get this man into trouble. He saved my life. Henry Champion planned to hang me. And the horse did go out from under me, but somebody cut me down before I could die. It had to be the man . . . the man in the dark, like you said. It couldn't have been your father, because he was unconscious. And something came to me a few minutes ago, Judy. When I came back to consciousness again, the body of the man who had been shot in the clearing was gone. Somebody had taken him away. It must have been the man in the dark.''

''Why would he take away a dead man?''

''To hide him, I suppose. To protect himself.''

''Maybe he took the others away, too. Maybe they won't find them when they look.''

Ben knitted his brows. ''You know, Judy, you may be right. I hope you are. I don't want this man to get into trouble. What he did was a good thing. Those men deserved to die.''

''I know.''

''So you and me, we'll say nothing about that man, all right? I mean, it was dark. And you can't see people clearly in the dark, right? Maybe you just found an old knife blade on the ground, and cut yourself loose.''

''Right.''

''And I never saw any of those men who went into the woods actually get killed. And the one I did see get killed . . . maybe it was my imagination. I was on the back of a horse, about to be hanged. A man might imagine any number of things at a time like that. Right?''

''Right.''

''So I'm thinking, maybe I won't say anything at all about seeing anybody get shot. I might be wrong about it, you see, and I'd hate to be wrong about a thing like that.''

"You're right, Uncle Ben."

"Maybe we'll both just kind of not say too much about anything at all, huh?"

She smiled, very slightly. "Maybe we won't."

He hugged her. "I'm glad you're not hurt, Judy."

To his surprise, she kissed him on the cheek. "I'm glad you're not hurt, too. And the man in the dark. I hope he's not hurt."

"I have a feeling he's just fine."

"I think I want to eat my food now."

"You go right ahead, honey."

The Reverend Bray was at the door come morning. Haggard and weary, having not slept at all since his daughter was brought to him, he was nevertheless a happy man. His daughter had been found. He knocked on the door, and Ben answered.

"Hello, Reverend," he whispered raspily. "Come in. Is Deborah with you?"

"She's right here." Deborah stepped out from behind him. Ben gazed at her a few moments, still unused to seeing her in feminine dress. He wondered where she'd found the dress. Someone's castoff, perhaps. It was ragged and stained, but she made it look good anyway. "Deborah wanted to speak to you. She and I have been up all night, talking. Good talk."

"Please, come in." Ben stepped back and let them enter. "I'm sorry for looking like I do. I been sleeping on that sofa yonder. The others are all still in bed. The doctor gave Jake and Sally something that pretty much knocked them out."

"How's your neck?" Bray asked.

Ben gingerly touched the red, tender place where the rope had bruised him. "Sore. And my voice ain't the same. But the doctor tells me no real harm was done."

They sat down. Ben could hardly keep his eyes off Deborah, and yet found it hard to keep them on her at the same time. She was the same, but not the same. A stranger now, even more so than before.

"Deborah has something she wants to tell you," Reverend Bray said.

Ben looked her in the face and waited.

"Ben . . . I told you false things before. Stories about my brother, and my father being dead. They weren't true."

"I know. Your father already explained things."

"But I want to tell you myself. I didn't really lie to you, because what I told you, I thought it all was true. My mind, you see . . . things aren't right. With my mind."

Ben smiled because he didn't know what else to do. "You seem fine right now."

"Yes . . . for now. It's been that way with me. There are times when everything is clear. The clear times last for a long time, sometimes. Then the clouds come. From somewhere. And I start to believe in things again that aren't true."

Ben knew nothing about mental illness. What could he say to her? "Maybe this time the clouds won't come back at all."

"We may only hope and pray," the reverend murmured.

She lowered her head. "Sometimes, when the clear times come, I don't remember all of what happened when the clouds were there. But this time I remember one thing. The fire."

Ben was sure she was about to admit to him that she set the blaze. He didn't want to hear it. He didn't want to associate this lovely woman with the death of Roscoe Hammel. "Deborah, please . . . if you're going to say what I'm afraid you are, I'd rather not know."

"Do you think I'm going to tell you that I set the fire? I'm not. Because I don't know. I remember the fire, but I don't know how it began. It's not clear . . . the clouds are there. But I'm afraid . . . afraid it was me. Because I've done it before, in my worst times. There have been other fires."

"Listen to me. You don't know how that fire began. I don't know. Nobody does. You can't assume you caused it."

"But neither can I be sure I didn't."

"So what are you thinking of doing?"

Reverend Bray cleared his throat and answered in her place. "We don't know what to do. Who can we turn to? Am I to take my own daughter to the law and tell them that maybe she was the cause of a fire that killed a man? It would be wrong to do that without being sure. Yet do we not owe it to that poor man who died to open up every possibility to examination?"

"To what end? Roscoe can't be brought back."

"Yes, but—"

"There is nothing for you to do now, Reverend, but to take care of your daughter, speak only what you know really *is*, as opposed to what merely might be, and to, well . . . pray. You ought to be familiar with that process. Pray. Ask that the truth come out, so that you can quit wondering."

"You honestly believe we are under no obligation to voice our suspicion to the authorities?"

"I honestly do." Ben pondered how strange it was to have a preacher, of all things, come to him for moral advice.

"Then we'll take your advice. We'll keep quiet for now, and pray for the truth to be told. Whatever it may be. And when it is . . . then we'll deal with it."

Ben smiled. "I think that's the wisest course."

"Yes. Thank you for your counsel. And for all your help lately, and . . . before. When Deborah was still, as she says, clouded."

"No thanks needed. But, Reverend . . . there's something you can do for me."

"You merely have to name it, sir."

"When you're doing that praying, also pray for a fellow I know, I don't want to say his name, who might need some protection. Pray for this fellow, if you would. That he'll not find trouble for a thing that he did."

"A bad thing?"

"No. A good thing."

Bray nodded. "We'll remember your friend, Mr. Woolard. Just as you ask."

* * *

The marshal arrived an hour later, throwing around questions in an irritable and almost accusatory fashion. Who did the kidnapping? Where are they now? What did they mean, Henry Champion the bushwhacker really was alive? That was the same talk that crazy gold-toothed black boy had talked. Did they not know that a man of the law had no time to waste on foolishness?

When the marshal was gone, Jake shook his head. "So much for all those notions of this fellow being the peace officer Ferguson needs. I believe maybe the way he handles his cases is just to complain about having them, accuse all the witnesses, then ignore it."

"Let him ignore it," Ben said.

"What? You don't want to get to the bottom of this? You don't want to see justice administered to those men?"

Ben stood. "I believe it likely that it already has."

The first of Reverend Bray's prayers was answered the next day. He held a copy of the latest newspaper edition in his hand and wept as he read the story: A local drunk had confessed to starting the fire that destroyed the Cathedral of Rest and took the life of one Roscoe Hammel. The motive as yet remained unclear, but evidence backing up the confession had been found and the man was in custody, awaiting indictment.

Ben saw off Bray and Deborah later the same day. They did not wish to linger in Ferguson any longer than they had to now that the only matter holding them was eliminated.

"What will you do for her?" Ben quietly asked the preacher, out of Deborah's earshot.

"All that I can," he replied. "There are new things being learned about the human mind, I'm told. People who can perhaps help her to keep those clouds of hers away. But I'm under no illusions. She's done this before, moving from insanity to lucidity, all in the snap of a finger. But it has never lasted. Always she goes back. Always there are more clouds."

Ben looked at her, perched on a wagon the preacher had

hired to convey himself and his daughter out of the mountains. She was a lovely lady, appealing despite the storm that he knew brewed inside her. He thought briefly of what might have been had circumstances, both his and hers, been different. Then he put out his hand and shook that of Reverend Bray.

"God go with you, sir, and keep the clouds away forevermore."

"Amen, my friend. Amen."

Ben watched the wagon rumble away, then turned back toward the house, feeling for the moment quite sad, and quite lost in clouds of his own.

Chapter Twenty-three

Ben heard the tapping on his window and sat up. A storm had swept in, lightning flashing, wind rattling shutters and making the roof creak, but the sound he had heard was not the result of the weather.

As he squinted toward the window, a lightning flash revealed something there, an object that moved and fluttered.

He rose and opened the window, momentarily letting in rain and wind. Retrieving what he had seen, he closed the window again, cranked up the lamp that burned low beside the sofa upon which he slept, and read the soggy note he had just snared. It had been pinned in place on the windowsill beneath a fist-size stone.

Ben did not lie down again for the duration of the night. When the note had dried, he lit it in the lamp and let it burn to ash on the hearth.

When Sally rose to cook breakfast, the storm was past and Ben's sofa was empty. He had dressed and left with the first light of dawn.

Walking on this particular terrain gave Ben a very troubling feeling. He looked about, seeing the place by daylight for the first time. There was the mule pen, empty now. Apparently the marshal and his deputies had removed all livestock since there was no one seemingly about to see to its care. There was the tree, with the rope that had hanged him still swinging from the limb. It looked quite innocent now, nothing to gain anyone's attention. After all, many folks in these mountains hung their foodstuffs in sacks from ropes just like that, to keep them out of reach of animals.

The place where Masker had died revealed no bloodstains. Someone had stirred the dirt considerably and managed to mask them all. As for any bodies being found close by, there had been none that Ben had heard of. Someone had removed them. The same someone, Ben was sure, who had made Masker's corpse vanish, and who had left the note on the windowsill a few hours before.

Ben stood in the middle of Henry Champion's claim and wondered what had become of the old bushwhacker. He'd fled in pure fright into the night, then vanished as if the earth had swallowed him.

"Ben."

The voice startled him, though he had been expecting it. He turned. "Howdy, Roanie."

"You doing all right, sir?"

"I'm fine, thank you."

Roanie Platt looked closely at him. "What happened to your neck?"

Ben narrowed his eyes. "I kind of figured you knew what had happened to my neck. How somebody strung me up from that tree yonder the other night, and then somebody else cut me down in time to save my life. Yes, sir, I figured you'd already know all about that."

"How would I know that, sir, unless I'd been close by to see it?"

So now they understood each other, and how this conversation was to progress from here on out. Nothing said directly, words carefully chosen, some things mutually known but mutually unspoken. Ben agreed with that approach. Better that way, in case the marshal ever should decide to do his job after all, and launch a true investigation.

"Good point, Roanie. I suppose you don't know a thing about what happened here at that."

"Only what I've heard, sir, from this man I talked to."

"What'd that man have to say?"

"He said there was a bunch of men killed hereabouts the other night. Said there'd been some poor little girl took prisoner to lure some others up here after her so they could be killed. But this man, he'd been watching this here claim close for some reason. Spying out them who worked it. When he seen them two men coming up unarmed, he fell in behind. Followed. This man, he seen what was going on, and decided he might ought to help out. He got the little girl free, this man did, and that drew a whole gang of bad men into the dark, after him."

"And what happened after that?" Ben asked.

"This man I talked to . . . he hinted around to me that maybe he killed them bad men, one at a time. Out in the dark. Didn't say it to me direct. Just hinted. And then, later on, maybe this man gathered up all the dead ones and nid them where they'll never be found."

"I see."

"Yes, sir. And I'm thinking that maybe it was this man who cut the rope you was hanging from."

"If that's the case, then I owe this man my thanks," Ben said. "You'll tell him for me, won't you, if you see him again?"

"I surely will, sir. But this man, I won't be seeing him. He's long gone now, sir. Long gone. Miles and miles away."

Ben nodded. "And what about you, Roanie? You planning to maybe leave, too, like this man did?"

"Maybe, sir. Maybe that'd be a good thing. You know, there's always folks who want to stir up trouble. Like marshals and such. Poking around, stirring up things, accusing folks of this and that that they don't know nothing about."

Ben said, "You know, that man you were talking about might have been worried that somebody would stir up trouble for him. Accuse him of something. Maybe that's why he left.''

"Maybe so, sir.''

"Too bad he didn't know that the marshal and his deputies came up here and poked around and didn't find a blessed thing. No dead men at all. He hid them well. And from what I hear, the marshal doesn't have much heart to go poking any further. I hear he's not sure that anything happened up here at all, and don't much care even if anything did.''

"I suspect, sir, that this man would still have left even if he knowed that. He ain't the kind to take chances. And besides, maybe he just don't want to be around these parts no more. For personal reasons, you could say.''

"Makes sense to me.''

"Well, sir, I'm glad you and me run into each other. Funny how that just happened. Especially since this man told me there's something he'd like you in particular to know. Said you didn't need to worry about Henry Champion no more. He said he could promise you firm that Henry Champion won't never bother you nor nobody else ever again.''

"That's good news. I wonder how it is that this man could know something like that?''

"Sir, I wouldn't know. Sure as the world, I wouldn't. Maybe this man tracked down Henry Champion in the dark after he run off, and took care of him.''

"Maybe he did.''

Roanie tipped his hat. "Well, sir, I believe I'll be going my way now. Don't expect we'll see each other again.''

"I'm glad I got to know you, Roanie. Mighty glad.''

"Me, too, sir. Good-bye.'' Roanie turned and began walking away, up toward the Goatbeard.

"Roanie . . . wait. If you were to see this man again, the one who cut my hanging rope, and if you were to ask him for me how Ben Woolard could know for absolute certain that Henry Champion was gone, what do you think this man would say?''

"I believe, sir, that he might say there was an old abandoned mine claim up two miles beyond that there Goat-beard peak. I believe he'd tell Ben Woolard to maybe go pay a visit there sometime.''

"Maybe Ben Woolard will do just that. Good-bye, Roanie. And thank you.''

"Ain't no reason to be thanking me, sir. I ain't done a thing. Not one thing.''

He turned again and walked away. Ben watched him until he was out of sight.

This was one of those claims that obviously had not come to much, for it had been abandoned early. Ben, winded from the long trek, looked the place over, puffing hard, hurting in every joint and every bruise—and of these he had plenty.

A shed stood nearby and he looked inside, holding his breath. Nothing. It was empty. An examination of every hole and crevice and nook failed to reveal anything of Henry Champion at all. Ben stood frowning, wondering if he'd come to the wrong place, or if Roanie had deliberately misdirected him.

He sat down and rested for almost an hour. He still hadn't adjusted fully to this thin, anemic high-mountain air. Pulling in big lungfuls of air, he tried to satisfy his body's craving for oxygen.

And in the process he caught a foul whiff of something. The breeze had shifted. He stood, wrinkling his nose and frowning. Quite a stench. Looking into the wind, he saw that it was blowing toward him over the mouth of the mineshaft.

A miner's "gallows" stood over the shaft. And from it, a rope descended into the dark hole. A rope not hanging loosely, as would be expected at an abandoned claim, but pulled tight.

Ben advanced to the shaft. The stench grew stronger. Something dead and decaying. Or someone.

He looked into the shaft and saw only black shadows. Testing the rope, he found that indeed there was something quite heavy at the unseen end of it, stretching it tight.

Ben put his hand to the pulley crank and began to work. The rope inched up slowly, heavily weighted. He had to stop and rest three times before at last the job was done.

Henry Champion's back was toward Ben when his body finally emerged from the shadows. Ben fixed the pulley in place and backed away, hand over his mouth and nose. The smell was terrible, making him want to retch.

Ben stared at Champion's back for a few moments, then circled the shaft to see the face. An ugly, blackened face, eyes half open and sunken, lips swollen and drawn back, revealing the interior of the mouth.

Ben looked close, and winced. Every tooth had been pulled out of Henry Champion's head.

Ben shook his head. "Roanie, I wonder why that man you met went and did a thing like that. I surely do wonder."

Ben pulled out his folding knife. Placing one hand over his mouth and nose again, he advanced toward the hanging body of the late Henry Champion, reached out, and sawed the rope in two. Champion's blackened corpse dropped into the shaft below him.

Ben Woolard folded and pocketed his knife, and turned his steps toward Ferguson and home.

BACK TO MALACHI

ROBERT J. CONLEY
THREE-TIME SPUR
AWARD-WINNER

Charlie Black is a young half-breed caught between two worlds. He is drawn to the promise of the white man's wealth, but torn by his proud heritage as a Cherokee. Charlie's pretty young fiancée yearns for the respectability of a Christian marriage and baptized children. But Charlie can't forsake his two childhood friends, Mose and Henry Pathkiller, who live in the hills with an old full-blooded Indian named Malachi. When Mose runs afoul of the law, Charlie has to choose between the ways of his fiancée and those of his friends and forefathers. He has to choose between surrender and bloodshed.

___4277-0 $3.99 US/$4.99 CAN

INCIDENT at BUFFALO CROSSING

ROBERT J. CONLEY

The Sacred Hill. It rose above the land, drawing men to it like a beacon. But the men who came each had their own dreams. There is Zeno Bond, the settler who dreams of land and empire. There is Mat McDonald, captain of the steamship *John Hart*, heading the looming war between the Spanish and the Americans. And there is Walker, the Cherokee warrior called by a vision he cannot deny—a vision of life, death...and destiny.

___4396-3 $4.50 US/$5.50 CAN

The Dark Brand

H. A. DeRosso

Driscoll made a mistake and he's paying for it. They stuck him in a cell—with a man condemned to hang the next morning. Driscoll learns how his cellmate robbed a bank and killed a man...and how the money was never recovered. But he never learns where the money is. After Driscoll serves his time and drifts back into town, he learns that the loot is still hidden, and that just about everyone thinks the condemned man told Driscoll where it is buried before he died. Suddenly it seems everybody wants that money—enough to kill for it.

___4412-9 $4.50 US/$5.50 CAN

BLACK RIVER FALLS
ED GORMAN

"Gorman's writing is strong, fast and sleek as a bullet. He's one of the best."
—Dean Koontz

Who would want to kill a beautiful young woman like Alison...and why? But whatever happens, nineteen-year-old Ben Tyler swears that he will protect her. It hasn't been easy for Ben–the boy the other kids always picked on. But then Ben finds Alison and at last things are going his way...Until one day he learns a secret so ugly that his entire life is changed forever. A secret that threatens to destroy everyone he loves. A secret as dark and dangerous as the tumbling waters of Black River Falls.

"Gorman has a way of getting into his characters and they have a way of getting into you."
—Robert Block, author of *Psycho*

——4265-7 $4.99 US/$5.99 CAN

Dorchester Publishing Co., Inc.
P.O. Box 6640
Wayne, PA 19087-8640

Please add $1.75 for shipping and handling for the first book and $.50 for each book thereafter. NY, NYC, and PA residents, please add appropriate sales tax. No cash, stamps, or C.O.D.s. All orders shipped within 6 weeks via postal service book rate. Canadian orders require $2.00 extra postage and must be paid in U.S. dollars through a U.S. banking facility.

Name_____
Address_____
City_____ State_____ Zip_____
I have enclosed $_____ in payment for the checked book(s).
Payment <u>must</u> accompany all orders. ❑ Please send a free catalog.

BRANDISH

DOUGLAS HIRT

FIRST TIME IN PAPERBACK!

Captain Ethan Brandish has finally given up his command of Fort Lowell, deep in Apache territory. But the vicious Apache leader, Yellow Shirt, has another fate in store for him. He and a group of renegade warriors attack a stage station and ride off just before Brandish arrives. But the Apaches are still out there—watching and waiting—and Brandish must risk his own life to save the few wounded survivors.

___4323-8 $4.50 US/$5.50 CAN

DARK TRAIL

Hiram King

When the War Between the States was finally over, many men returned from battle only to find their homes destroyed and their families scattered to the wind. Bodie Johnson is one of those men. But while some families fled before advancing armies, the Johnson family was packed up like cattle and shipped west—on a slave train. With only that information to go on, Bodie sets out to find whatever remains of his family. And he will do it. Because no matter how vast the West is, no matter what stands in his way, Bodie knows one thing—the Johnsons will survive.

___4418-8 $5.50 US/$6.50 CAN

Dorchester Publishing Co., Inc.
P.O. Box 6640
Wayne, PA 19087-8640

Please add $1.75 for shipping and handling for the first book and $.50 for each book thereafter. NY, NYC, and PA residents, please add appropriate sales tax. No cash, stamps, or C.O.D.s. All orders shipped within 6 weeks via postal service book rate. Canadian orders require $2.00 extra postage and must be paid in U.S. dollars through a U.S. banking facility.

Name_____
Address_____
City_____State_____Zip_____
I have enclosed $_____ in payment for the checked book(s).
Payment <u>must</u> accompany all orders. ❏ Please send a free catalog.
CHECK OUT OUR WEBSITE! www.dorchesterpub.com

DANGER RIDGE
TIM MCGUIRE

Clay Cole is a man with a shadowy past. Most folks know he is good with a gun, but that is all they know. Very few know the Army is out to court-martial him for something he didn't do. And even fewer know he has accepted a job to lead a young bride along a dangerous trail to meet her husband. But the men who do know it are aiming to kill him and the woman along the trail. And the easiest place to do that is the treacherous sort few men make it through—the place the Westerners call danger ridge.

___4410-2 $4.50 US/$5.50 CAN

Dorchester Publishing Co., Inc.
P.O. Box 6640
Wayne, PA 19087-8640

Please add $1.75 for shipping and handling for the first book and $.50 for each book thereafter. NY, NYC, and PA residents, please add appropriate sales tax. No cash, stamps, or C.O.D.s. All orders shipped within 6 weeks via postal service book rate. Canadian orders require $2.00 extra postage and must be paid in U.S. dollars through a U.S. banking facility.

Name_____
Address_____
City_____ State_____ Zip_____
I have enclosed $_____ in payment for the checked book(s).
Payment <u>must</u> accompany all orders. ❑ Please send a free catalog.
    CHECK OUT OUR WEBSITE! www.dorchesterpub.com